MURPHY

Other books by Kurt Unkelbach

LOVE ON A LEASH

THE WINNING OF WESTMINSTER

THE DOG IN MY LIFE

MURPHY

KURT UNKELBACH

PRENTICE-HALL, INC., ENGLEWOOD CLIFFS, N.J.

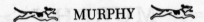 MURPHY

by Kurt Unkelbach

© 1967 by KURT UNKELBACH

LIBRARY OF CONGRESS CATALOG CARD NUMBER: 67-16394

PRINTED IN THE UNITED STATES OF AMERICA

T60680

PRENTICE-HALL INTERNATIONAL, INC., LONDON
PRENTICE-HALL OF AUSTRALIA, PTY. LTD., SYDNEY
PRENTICE-HALL OF CANADA, LTD., TORONTO
PRENTICE-HALL OF INDIA PRIVATE LTD., NEW DELHI
PRENTICE-HALL OF JAPAN, INC., TOKYO

To Hedy and Dean White

Nobody knows the number of wild dogs and semi-wild dogs in this country today, but they exist in the millions.

Most were once pets and some still are, and they are found almost everywhere: suburbs, countryside, resort areas and even cities.

This is the story of several such dogs, and of one dog in particular—Murphy, a Beagle.

❧❧ ❧❧ ONE ❧❧ ❧❧

THE SMILE ON THE BOY'S face spread into a satisfied grin. This was the happiest day that he could remember.

His name was Henry Deane. A redheaded teenager who desperately wanted a dog of his own and had resolved that the dog must be a Beagle. Now, after a long search, he had found his Beagle. His father's field glasses gave the boy the feeling that he could reach out and touch the pup.

From his vantage point in the giant oak tree, a hundred yards from the old barn foundation on the deserted Thompson farm, Henry watched as the Beagle and two friends—a big black dog and a yellow one—emerged from their hideout and trotted across the field and into the woods. Not a single one had a collar.

They were pack dogs, but Henry didn't know it. He was fairly certain that the Beagle pup was homeless, and very sure that the little hound was just the one he wanted. Only one small problem remained: How to capture the Beagle?

1

The boy was confident that he could solve the problem. Hadn't he proved himself to be as talented as an Indian scout? No one had pointed out the tracks on the bank of the stream—he had discovered them! Some of those tracks were small and round, the pads firm and clearly defined, just like the ones Art Purdy had drawn for him; and he alone deduced that those small tracks, among the big ones, belonged to a Beagle.

Ten minutes after the pack had departed, the boy was still up in the tree. Then he remembered the day: Sunday, and he had promised his mother that he would be home for dinner at one o'clock. He glanced at his wristwatch. Fifteen minutes to one. If he hurried, he could make it and thus escape a sure lecture from his father concerning responsibility, duty and honor.

Henry felt enormously pleased as he lowered himself from branch to branch and finally to the base of the tree. Once on the ground, he raised the glasses to his eyes and studied the old barn foundation. Somewhere there the Beagle and the other dogs lived, and the boy decided to become their friend. It was a logical first step to winning the trust of the Beagle.

"I'll be back later this afternoon," Henry promised the absent dogs. A squirrel scolded from a nearby hickory. "You should hear my father scold. He could give you a lesson," the boy said to the squirrel.

Henry turned and walked to the dirt road. Then he ran down the road toward his home.

Weeks before, on the first Tuesday in September, the Beagle pup had spent the morning hours following a man

2

and a woman from their cottage to the car and back again to the cottage. They were loading their car for the trip back to the city and the Beagle pup was anxious to help—but all Murphy could do was trot back and forth because there was nothing small enough to carry in his mouth.

Once, when the man carried a mattress out of the cottage he really couldn't see where he was going and he almost tripped and fell because Murphy was in the way. The man kicked at the hound pup and swore at him and Murphy stayed close to the woman after that.

Finally, when all the clothes, cartons, and sheets and blankets were jammed into the car, and the mattress was tied on top, the man settled into the driver's seat and lit a cigar. After awhile the woman came out of the cottage. She was stout and she took her time as she closed and locked the door and then walked to the car and got into it.

Murphy backed off about ten feet and sat down. The pup cocked his head and watched the woman. He had not been in the car since his arrival in June, but now he rather expected an invitation, for the people had put just about everything into the car except him. He barked just once and the woman looked at him.

"I think he knows," she said.

"He's too dumb to know anything. Now what did you forget? I don't want to get all the way to the city before you remember that you forgot something."

"We have everything," she assured her husband. "I wish we could keep Murphy."

"Now don't start that again. You knew when we bought him that we couldn't have him in the apartment. The farmer said he'd give the mutt a good home, so stop worrying. He'll be over later to pick him up."

3

"But will Murphy wait here?"

"Sure he'll wait. This is the only home he knows."

"Maybe we should phone the farmer. What's his name?"

"How do I know? I bought eggs from him a couple of times this summer. I don't go around asking farmers their names." Then the man turned on the ignition and called to Murphy, "So long, slob. You've had your vacation. Take care of yourself." He slipped the car into gear and stepped on the gas. The pup sat there and watched as the blue-thing-on-wheels rolled down the lane and around the curve and out of view.

The man was lying. He had not talked to the farmer, nor to anyone else, about giving Murphy a home.

For the rest of that day, Murphy waited at the cottage for his family. The pup had no way of knowing that the man and the woman would not return and that he had been abandoned.

He was just over seven months of age, and almost as big as he was ever going to be: Fourteen inches at the withers and twenty-two pounds. All in all, he was a handsome fellow, and only a breed expert would have faulted him for too high a tail set. The pup's saddle was black over deep tan, and the stockings on all four legs were uniform, with the white extending up over the fore of his deep chest. His big, brown eyes were set well apart, and his expression was soft and pleading, even modest—as if he were aware of his fine hound qualities, but preferred not to brag.

Ever since June, when they bought him at the city pet shop, the couple and Murphy lived together at the cottage by the lake. Not *in* the cottage, for at the man's insistence, Murphy was not permitted indoors. But sometimes the man was compelled to return to the city to work for a few days, and on such occasions the woman invited Murphy into the cottage and shared the sanctuary with him.

Murphy, of course, preferred these periods when he and the woman were alone. He was permitted to sleep in the bed on the man's side. But when the man was there, the pup slept on a bed of dried grass and leaves under the front stoop.

And when the man was away, the woman and the dog often took short walks through the woods and the fields. Sometimes they got as far as the next cottage, where a pleasant lady-artist lived with only a pair of Manx cats for companions. The cats were not afraid of Murphy, and he enjoyed their society, especially when they did not finish their dinner. When they were not watching, he was only too happy to finish it for them.

For the woman who had wanted a dog as a companion, "up in that wild wilderness" sixty miles from the city; and for the man and Murphy, it was a rather uneventful summer. Not a single wild bear or wolf appeared to threaten the stout woman, so Murphy was not called upon to protect her, and he performed his duty well. She did not teach him any cute tricks or many commands. He filled her lonely hours, and this companionship was all that she asked of him. He was fed twice daily, plus tidbits at odd hours, for the woman was forever feeding herself.

Only on one occasion did she treat the dog unkindly. It happened when she and Murphy were walking through the woods, and a baby rabbit hopped across their path. Murphy caught it. The accomplishment was no great feat—the bunny was hardly more than two weeks free from the warren. Still, the little gray thing was a treasure to Murphy and he wanted to share it.

5

The thought of killing the rabbit did not enter his mind. He had simply picked it up between his strong jaws, waited until it stopped struggling, then carried the limp body back to the woman.

The woman was horrified. She held Murphy by his slack neck skin and hit him with her free hand until he dropped the rabbit. Then she picked him up, scolded him, and spanked him as if he were a baby. He did not understand her words and the blows did not really hurt him; but, from the tone of her voice and her actions, he felt that he had done something wrong. When she dropped him to the ground, he crouched at her feet and whimpered, although his tail did not stop wagging.

Then she hurried back to the cottage. Murphy waited a decent interval before following. When he did, he found the woman talking to the man. As Murphy approached them, the man turned and shouted, "Come here, you little murderer!"

Murphy had no idea what the word "murderer" meant, but he soon found out. The man batted him several times across the muzzle and ears and then sent him sprawling with a mighty kick to the hindquarters. Then the man laughed.

Since that time, the woman had not treated him unkindly. He liked her but he didn't care for the man, because the man had abused him several times since the bunny incident. Murphy more or less tolerated him.

Now, as he confidently awaited the return of his family, Murphy was truly alone in the world, a new orphan entirely dependent upon his own wits for survival, and completely unaware of his predicament. Not a very promising situation for a puppy who looked older and wiser than he really was.

If someone, somehow, could have made the little dog understand that his aloneness was not unique, it would not have helped him. All across America during that September, wherever humans were leaving their vacation retreats for their permanent homes in the cities, pets were being abandoned by the tens of thousands. It is an annual September folly practiced by civilized people, many of whom go to church, pay taxes and obey most laws. Dogs and cats and parakeets and rabbits and goats and even ponies—pets acquired for the summer, often for the benefit of children—are tossed out of the lives of people as thoughtlessly as they toss beer cans from windows of their speeding cars. It is a cruel, senseless thing to do but it is a very real thing, and it happened to Murphy.

Always before, it had just been a question of waiting. He was so sure that the man and the woman would return, and his belief was helped by a full belly: Two cans of food instead of one, plus several strips of bacon, five frankfurters, a sugar doughnut and three stale rolls.

So he was well fed, and he slept soundly under the stoop that first night. He was a little hungry by the next afternoon, but not ravenous. It was a warm day, and satisfying his thirst was no problem, for the lake was nearby.

There was a slight gnawing feeling in his stomach as the darkness came again. He wanted to sleep on top of the stoop so that he could bark an immediate welcome as soon as the man and woman returned. But midnight brought rain, and he retired to his dry quarters under the stoop.

When morning came and he found his family still absent,

Murphy decided to relieve his real hunger somehow. He remembered the large can at the rear of the cottage and trotted off to inspect the possibilities. He had often seen the woman dump remnants of a meal into that can, and the stranger who had emptied it into his truck had not been around for some time.

The can was still there, and his nose told him that food of sorts was in it. Even standing on his hind legs, he could not reach the top—and if that had been possible, the lid with a rock on top of it would have thwarted him.

Murphy backed off, sat down, and considered the problem. A bird could have told him that the lid was rusted and not a tight fit, and that was why the scent of rotting table scraps was so strong. The scent increased his feeling of hunger. He stood up and pawed at the can, then he leaned against it. The can did not budge.

He remembered a similar can that stood outside the lady-artist's cottage, and that brought back fond memories of her cats and their dinner dishes. He decided to pay the lady a visit, but first he walked around to the front of his own cottage and peered down the lane, just to make sure that the man and the woman had not returned. There was no sign of them.

It was almost the last time that he would think of the man and the woman. Oh, he would meet the woman again, but he could not know that. Now he trotted to the shore of the lake and followed the familiar path to the cottage of the nice lady with the Manx cats.

The cottage was shut tight for winter, with solid wooden storm doors front and rear, and the windows hidden behind board frames. The artist and her beloved cats had departed for the city some days before, and the rain had dispersed any human scent that was sometimes on the ground near her cottage.

The owner was the type of woman who could not resist a bargain and had never really estimated her worldly needs. As a result, she kept enough food on hand to feed a large family, although she ate sparingly and had no particular schedule for meals.

Otherwise, she was an orderly person. Behind the cottage, next to the very full garbage can, she had stacked several cardboard cartons, each full of items she had no future need for or did not want to carry back to the city. "My summer's end pile" she called it. Sooner or later it would be removed by the private garbage collector when he made his final rounds of the summer cottages.

The cartons contained a variety of things, from empty paint tubes and old brushes to dust rags, magazines, letters, rotten vegetables, spoiled lamb chops, and empty sardine cans. After the lady's departure some animal or animals had knocked over the garbage can and ripped open the cartons. They had feasted on the edibles and spread the rest of it around the backyard.

Since Murphy had approached the front of the cottage, he did not immediately notice the rubbish on the ground. He went straight to the little front porch, barked to announce his arrival, and then sat down to await the appearance of his friends. It had worked before, but it didn't work this time. He barked again but to no avail. Then he remembered that the cats' dishes were usually found on the other side of the cottage, so he trotted around the cottage and came upon the scene of disarray.

9

Without even the slightest hesitation, he launched an item-by-item investigation and was delighted to discover an open sardine can that still contained a few drops of oil. He lapped up the oil, found the taste pleasant, and looked for another can. He found one, but it was upside down and he could not turn it over despite several attempts with his nose and front paws. But he did manage to push it near a heap of rags which covered a broiled chicken leg. It was no trouble for him to scent the leg, pull off the rags, and devour the leg—bone and all.

This trifle managed to increase rather than diminish his appetite, and he looked around for anything else that resembled food. He bit into the largest of several onions, but found the taste discouraging. Indeed, one swallow sent him galloping to the lake for a drink. When he returned to the mess on the ground, he located a paper bag of potato peels and devoured them. He chewed and swallowed a square piece of butcher paper that still carried the stain and the scent of meat.

There was nothing else around of edible interest. Murphy retired to the lake for another drink and then headed in the general direction of his own cottage. He was still hungry.

Midway on the return journey, his keen nose picked up a strong, strange scent. He paused and tilted his head upward and sniffed. He had passed the spot earlier, coming in the opposite direction, but the smell had not been there. A knowledgeable human being would have recognized the musky smell as similar to that of rotting cucumbers. And a native of the area, aware that cucumbers do not grow in rocks and brush, would have retreated in a hurry. The scent spelled copperheads—and danger.

Murphy found the scent interesting but hardly appetizing. Still, it seemed worth investigating. He moved some ten feet off the path, then paused to sniff again. The scent was much stronger. It was also less appealing. He retraced his steps to the path and continued homeward. The colony of copperheads uncoiled and relaxed and enjoyed the warmth of the flat rocks under the September sun.

On home grounds once more, Murphy headed directly for his private retreat under the stoop. Food was still on his mind, but the little he had enjoyed, combined with a great deal of water, dictated a nap.

A slight breeze swept through the yard and he moved with it; a circumstance that brought him within twenty-five feet of a bunny before he noticed its presence. Even then, if the three-month-old visitor—with the innocent inquisitiveness of youth—had not sat up on its haunches to view him, Murphy might not have noticed.

But he did, and the law of survival of the fittest prevailed. He bounded for the rabbit, and the long-eared thing raced for the cottage and disappeared under it. Space did not permit further pursuit.

Murphy returned to where the rabbit had been, and sniffed the ground. The scent was familiar and it bothered him. Somehow it dimly reminded him of the time he had been scolded and beaten and kicked by the stout woman and the man. It was the last time he would think of those two, but it discouraged any immediate plan to pursue the bunny.

The feeling of tiredness returned. He crept under the stoop and curled himself into a ball. It was early afternoon and chilly—soon he was asleep. He twitched as he slept and emitted little barks and growls. He was unhappier than he realized. Even more than food, he missed companionship.

❧❧ ❧❧ TWO ❧❧ ❧❧

THE MOON WAS FULL, AND the shores of the lake were bathed in a half blue light. The darkness was more of a haze, and the shapes of trees could be seen at a distance of thirty or forty feet. Murphy crawled out from under the stoop, feeling hungry and lonely and very stiff. He wriggled his body as if to loosen his backbone, then stretched his hind legs, first one and then the other. He shook his head several times, dismissing sleep from his eyes, and finally, he yawned.

He looked around, then stretched his head back, opened his mouth and howled. He had barked and whined and whimpered before, but it was the first time in his life that he had ever howled.

Pleased with this new sound, he tried it several times. He didn't know that his discovery was inherited. He assumed complete credit for its creation, and the assumption helped his ego. By this time, his ego really needed help.

He tried one more howl and gloried in its tone. Then he sat down and listened, for he was sure an answer would come from somewhere in the night. Moments later, an adolescent screech owl emitted a series of quavering ooo-ooo-ooos. The timing was probably a coincidence, but it gave Murphy courage to do some exploring into the world beyond his little world. Perhaps he would find food and companionship.

He trotted down the lane to a point along the straightway where ancient, crumbling stone walls lined both sides of the route. Since his arrival in June, he had not passed beyond this point. But he did so now, running as fast as he could until he reached the intersection of the lane and the secondary highway. He paused at the edge of the highway, not knowing which direction to choose. Far off in the hills, clusters of small lights gleamed in the darkness. One cluster went out as he watched. Suddenly the remaining lights became his immediate goal.

Lost in his own concentration, he started across the highway and found himself trapped in the blazing glare of two huge, white lights. A strange roar accompanied the lights. Murphy crouched.

A truck, racing by, missed him by ten feet. He was frightened. Then, from the opposite direction, two more glaring eyes sped toward him. Murphy jumped to his feet and ran for his life. Immediately behind him, brakes squealed and tires whined against the pavement. The car skidded crazily, and stopped. The driver, a man with a heart, got out of the car and looked around, but the dog had disappeared.

He returned to his car and drove off. "I'm still shaking," he said.

"You could have killed both of us," his passenger replied.

14

"A damn fool thing to do. You should have blasted right into that dog."

The driver did not reply. He knew all the rules for safe driving, and that it is wisest to step on the gas and not try to avoid hitting an animal. It was all sound advice but a life is a life.

"Maybe you hit him anyway," said the passenger. "He wasn't so big. We wouldn't have felt the bump. The car could have clipped him and thrown him fifty feet into the woods. Just because you didn't see his body doesn't mean you didn't hit him. So for all we know, you killed him while almost killing us."

"For God's sake, shutup!"

A frightened Murphy lay motionless in the drainage ditch on the opposite side of the highway. The car had barely scraped him, but the contact had added impetus to his blind flight and hurled him over the highway's shoulder and downgrade, head over heels, into the ditch. For several minutes, he remained motionless—in a state of shock. He did not know where he was, nor did he greatly care.

Finally, he twisted his head and licked the blood on his right thigh. The car had hit him, but the damage wasn't serious, nor would it hinder his movement in any way. His tongue was defense against infection, but the patch would be long in the healing and the scar would be there until the hard coat grew back to cover it.

When Murphy struggled to his feet, he had at least achieved his objective of crossing the road. But why had he wanted to cross it? The roaring motors above his head and the monsters with the glaring eyes didn't seem like friendly fellows to him.

To anyone but Murphy, his next move made little sense: He wanted to get back to the other side of the highway. This new world was not to his liking, and the only other world that he knew was back at the cottage.

The Beagle pup climbed the grade and looked in both directions. He saw no glaring lights. Then he crossed the highway, slowly as if to tempt fate. It took less than a minute—a blessed minute, strangely devoid of traffic.

He searched for the lane and found it, then started his journey homeward. He was tired. Sometimes he sat down and rested, but not too often; for whenever he sat, the aching hunger returned.

It was only a half mile to the cottage, but to Murphy it was the longest half mile of his life.

During his absence, visitors had arrived at the cottage. Canine visitors.

There were three of them, all full-grown and compared to Murphy they were giants.

One was an English Setter who answered to the name of Sport. Of the three, he was the only purebred, and the only one who wore a license tag. Another one, in his puppyhood, had known children who had called him Rover. He was bigger than the Setter, and his coat was long and golden. He was of mixed lineage, mostly Collie and Golden Retriever, with a head indicating a trace of Boxer.

And then there was King. In outline, King resembled a German Shepherd. Surely he counted at least one among his ancestors, but he was too outsized for the breed. He had a massive head and too long a body, with a curled tail reminiscent of sled dogs. His short, dense coat was coal black, which enhanced a general appearance of evil. He looked mean, and he was mean.

No one knew his origin. He had been seen in the county over a period of three years and had earned the name of King. The name suited him, for he was a leader in every sense—particularly a leader of pack dogs. Justly or unjustly, he was blamed for every canine atrocity in the area. When two offenses were committed by dogs at the same time, but twenty miles apart, his human critics did not find it inconsistent to put the blame on King.

There were individuals in the county who had sworn to get King. Some had spent days in their efforts to track him down. The attempts were futile, but there was always hope. The few who actually saw King agreed on one point: Somebody, somewhere, had come close to getting him, for his left ear wasn't much more than a stump.

These three were enjoying a feast of sorts as Murphy neared the cottage. They had knocked over the garbage can with the greatest of ease. The lid had been jarred off as it fell.

The stout woman had left all kinds of delicacies: Assorted odds and ends of cold cuts, partial loaves of stale bread, cooked vegetables, dill pickles, half a lemon meringue pie, a ham bone, the butt end of a roast, and old but flavorsome chocolates.

This was the fourth garbage can of the evening for the trio, and they dined in a leisurely fashion, for their appetites were no longer keen. Indeed, Sport had been well fed by his owner before nightfall, and at this time he was only interested in the pie. He did not find it much to his liking so he explored the yard while his companions continued to pick and choose from the discarded morsels on the ground. It was Sport who first noticed the homecoming Murphy.

The Setter growled and assumed a position of stiff attention. The Beagle pup, overjoyed to meet a fellow canine, trotted straight up to the stranger, tail wagging and spinal column wiggling. Murphy was delighted. He crouched before the rigid Sport and yipped his joy, then rolled on his back and pawed at the atmosphere in an obvious invitation to play. But Sport just stood there, completely unresponsive. He was awaiting directions from the leader.

King and Rover had heard the growl from the rear of the cottage. Both were tense when they appeared on the scene. Murphy was not aware of their presence until they were a few feet away. He scrambled to his feet, barked and leaped for King.

Sport and Rover backed off in horror, for they had seen King put more respectful dogs in their place. But this time he simply lowered his massive head, butted the off-balance pup to the ground, and with a front paw on Murphy to hold him down he sniffed the entire length of the pup's body.

Murphy did not move until the paw was withdrawn. A moment later, he scrambled to his feet, jumped and placed his forepaws on King's lowered head and busily licked the leader's muzzle. Sport and Rover sat and watched the performance, expecting savage trouble to break loose any minute. Their leader had been patient longer than usual.

Murphy's display of affection lasted about twenty seconds. King was more embarrassed than irritated; it might have been the first touch of affection he had ever experienced from man or beast.

The big dog shook the pup off and walked away. He

18

paused, turned his head and looked at Sport and Rover. Then he trotted around the cottage, went through the backyard and on toward the shore of the lake. His brief look had apparently contained a command, for both the Setter and the yellow dog hurried after him with never a glance back at the remaining morsels of food.

For Murphy, it was a surprising end to a pleasant few minutes. He was not sure if the trio would return and felt there was little wisdom in taking chances. He saw no point in being alone. His hunger for companionship was a real thing. He hesitated for a very few seconds, then ran off on the trail of the pack.

The trail led through the backyard where he discovered the morsels of old food. Lonely or not, his hunger was also very real, and he diligently devoured every bite that remained, including the lemon meringue pie. He did not like the taste of it, but this was no time to be particular.

When there was nothing more to eat, the need to satisfy his other hunger returned. Nose to the ground, he followed the trio's route to the lakeshore and along the path to the lady-artist's cottage. The pack had paused to investigate some rotting summer squash in the artist's tiny vegetable garden before proceeding on another path through the woods. Murphy was in a new world again, but somehow he felt confident and he did not even flinch when several grouse, roosting on a low limb, took off with a roaring whir as he passed underneath their perch. He alternated between walking and running and dismissed the thought of resting. Somewhere ahead, he knew he would find his new friends.

The trail led to the lakeshore again, and suddenly, he lost the scent. Murphy backtracked for several feet to make sure that he did not make a mistake. He returned to the point where the scent disappeared and investigated beyond it and into the adjacent woods. He went back to the shore, and lapped the water where it was shallow. Then for no reason at all, he stepped into the water until it tickled his belly. He stopped and lifted his head to the heavens and howled. When he howled a second time, it was too much for a nearby bullfrog. The frog leaped from his private lily pad, directly in front of the puppy. Murphy bounded in the direction of the splash and found himself swimming.

He kept right on swimming until his feet hit bottom and he walked on the shore of a small island. The scent of his friends was suddenly very strong. He was back on the trail—and he wasted no time following it past two cottages to a bridge that reached the far shore. He was tired, but his spirits had picked up—although he did not know, as King did, that the swim had saved him more than two miles on the long trip to his new home.

⚞ ⚞ THREE ⚞ ⚞

KING'S VISIT TO THE LAKE that night was the last he would make for many weeks. He had learned in other years that the cottages were deserted at this season, and that humans would visit the area only infrequently until the days turned warm again.

The visit was in the nature of a final reconnaissance, to make doubly sure that humans were not there. The raiding of the garbage cans was no more than a bit of sport. He and his cronies would need the area when the snow fell. Few of the cottages had cellars, and the crawl space under most provided ample shelter. He had used the lake area as his sanctuary for several winters. The tracks in the snow would go unnoticed, and a variety of hiding places, never used for more than a day at a time, would serve to confuse any seekers.

King could not reason why humans were absent in the

winter. It was enough for him to know that they would not be around. The fact that the lake was spring-fed, and thus not always safe for ice fishing or ice skating—and that the acreage was privately owned and posted against hunting— was of no interest to him. The ice would hold him and his pack, and that was sufficient. A fine escape route, if needed.

In other seasons, as now, his favorite abode was in a barn on a long-abandoned farm. The Thompson farmhouse had burned many years before, but the small barn had withstood weather and lightning for some years before it collapsed. The decayed floor beams had fallen, and in so doing had created a sheltered corner in the basement. The basement was there because the barn had been built into a steep rise of ground, and it opened to the south. It had been used as a wagon shed.

This shelter was the ultimate destination of King on the night he was followed by the Beagle. It was a little over six miles from the lake, as the crow flies, but King had led his pack on a circuitous route amounting closer to ten. He did this with the future in mind, an informal side trip to examine potential opportunities: Pastures where sheep and cows still grazed, henhouses and goat barns, rabbit hutches and even a kennel or two. He avoided homes and farms where pet dogs might bark, but he did not avoid kennels. When kennel dogs barked at night, their owners seldom troubled to investigate. King was not interested in the dogs themselves. He just wanted to make sure they were still there. They were his social inferiors, far too dependent on humans.

It was still a long way 'til dawn when he reached his hideaway and Rover was the only one with him. They had parted company with the Setter along the way, and Sport had retired to his own quarters in the woodshed on the property of his master, the county sheriff.

Sheriff Peter Long was a man of strong convictions. While he had never adequately trained or hunted Sport, he was convinced that his Setter was the best bird dog in seven counties. He was also convinced that a dog, no matter how dearly loved, should not be spoiled by permitting him to live in the house. Thus, after supper each evening, Sport was dismissed from the house and directed to go to bed in the woodshed.

Sport always did as directed, but in the past eight months he had remained there only until the lights went out in his master's house. Then he prowled around the countryside, hoping to find King, which he usually did. Thus, he was a part-time pack dog. He had first met King by accident and won his immediate acceptance by introducing the big black dog to the sheriff's henhouse and helping out with the slaughter. Sport disliked the chickens anyway, and the sheriff had taught him how to unlatch and open the henhouse door. "Smartest dog you ever saw," was Sheriff Long's proud boast to visitors. "Watch this. Be a good dog, Sport. Open the henhouse door. Go ahead, show how smart you are."

Murphy plodded along through the night, concentrating on following the pack's trail. His only moments of fear came when the trail approached a major highway and he could see the monsters with the blazing eyes speeding past. And then he learned how to safely avoid the monsters by going through a culvert. He could do it merely by walking. King and Rover and Sport had succeeded previously on their bellies.

At several points, he noted that one of his new acquaintances had branched off from the others. Each time, he followed the trail of two, and sure enough, each time the single dog rejoined the other two along the route.

He tarried only once, and that was alongside a low building with attached wire runs. On the other side of the wire, twenty Poodles started to bark at him, and Murphy barked right back. He would have loved to stay and play with them, but could find no opening in the wire. After a while, he noticed that the Poodles were barking at each other and not at him. Then the lights were turned on in a house nearby, and the night was suddenly filled with shrill whistles and angry human voices.

Murphy put his nose to the ground, picked up the trail again, and departed from the confusion.

Near the home of Sheriff Long, the scent of one dog branched off from those of the other two. Murphy followed the double, as usual, and when the single scent did not rejoin the others later, he was not concerned.

At dawn he reached the abandoned farm and what was left of the old barn. King and Rover, not born to the wild—but wild in alertness—sensed his coming when he was still a hundred yards away. They were fully awake, poised for fight or flight, when Murphy appeared in the basement.

The two big dogs looked at Murphy, yawned and relaxed. Then they retreated to the dark corner under the fallen beams and curled up on the ground to continue their sleep.

Murphy walked up to King and licked his good ear and was rewarded with a grunt. Then he curled himself as close to King as possible and succumbed to sleep himself.

Pack dogs, delinquent dogs, bad dogs. They are known by many names. Country children call them "night dogs," and that's close enough, for most of their work is done at night. The work consists mostly of finding something to eat.

Night dogs are usually big and strong and fast and smart. The odds against a Beagle becoming a night dog—or even being accepted by other night dogs—would be something like one-in-a-million.

Murphy was one-in-a-million.

Art Purdy would have agreed with those odds.

No man in Green Valley knew more about Beagles than big, good-natured Art, owner and staff of the service station. He considered his career an ideal one, for he liked dealing with people almost as much as he loved hounds, and hunting, and fishing, and the telling of tall tales. While people were not his main interest in life, he certainly didn't neglect them, and there were those who said that Green Valley would never need a newspaper as long as Art Purdy was around.

He was the last person in the village to talk to Murphy's family. They had stopped at the station for gasoline on the way home to the city, and all of the conversation had been supplied by Art: "Fill her up?" and "That will be three-eighty" and "Thanks. See you next summer." The man had grunted each time, and the woman hadn't looked at the man or at Art.

Just a routine business transaction, and Art forgot all about it until his young friend Henry Deane dropped in for a visit. The boy was on his way home from school, and Art was glad to see him. He saved his tallest stories for Henry, who had been a city boy most of his life and seemed willing to believe anything. "You might say he's short for his age, which is thirteen, and old for his years, also thirteen," was the way Art had once described Henry to his wife. "First red-head without freckles I've ever seen. Can't keep his hair combed, always wears a tie, and I've never known a more polite kid. Doesn't say much, but he sure can listen."

On this afternoon, Art took one look at the boy's somber expression and asked, "Why are you looking so happy? Do you like the idea that school has started again?"

"I don't dislike it, Sir," said Henry. "How are your dogs?"

"Fine. Say, seeing you reminds me of something. You know that city couple who bought the Bartlett cottage at the lake? Well, they were here Tuesday. Headed back to the city, and their car was piled sky high with everything they owned—except for their dog, now that I think about it. If I'm any judge of character, Henry, those people are the sort of idiots who think a pup can live off the land. Follow me?"

"No, Sir. I don't know the people, either."

"Now listen carefully, Henry. I've got a hunch that they just turned that pup loose. Summer people do that all the time. Reason I'm telling you this is because the pup is a Beagle. Nice little fellow. Used to watch me from the bank when I was plugging for bass this summer. He'd be just right for you, Henry. Now do you follow me?"

Henry grinned, nodded and said, "I'll be at the lake in the morning. Which cottage do they own?"

Art drew a rough map of the near side of the lake and showed Henry the precise location of the cottage. "Of course, if they left him there, he could be wandering anywhere around the lake. So if he's not at the cottage, look around for tracks on soft ground. Here, this is what Beagle tracks look like. Round and small, see? No school tomorrow?"

"Tomorrow is Saturday," Henry reminded him. "Thanks

26

for telling me about the Beagle. You don't think they gave the dog to somebody?"

"Wouldn't I have heard by now? Besides, I can look at a man and tell if he's an animal lover or not. This man hates himself. Good luck."

Henry was so excited that he ran most of the way home. His want for a dog predated his family's move to Green Valley the year before—Green Valley, where all the other boys seemed to own dogs. His great wish went all the way back to his final years in the city, and even now he could quote his father's stock reply: "A dog would not be happy in the city, Henry. Perhaps we'll move to the country someday, and then you'll have your dog. I promise."

He was the loneliest boy in Green Valley. No one was really at fault, but that's the way it was. Henry had never found it easy to make new friends of his own age, and his natural reserve was quite often mistaken for standoffishness. The boy had nothing in common with his new contemporaries, and they did not go out of their way to establish friendships with the new kid from the city. They misunderstood him, and when he proved to be a good student, they misunderstood him more. His ninth-grade classmates regarded him with suspicion. Who did Henry Deane think he was?

Time had turned the lonely boy's desire into obsession, and a dog had become more important to him than anything else in life. It went beyond companionship and something of his own to love, though he still held to those normal dreams. The dog had developed into a symbol of acceptance, a key to unlock the hearts of others, the proof that Henry Deane was indeed a regular fellow. He was so sure of all that, but even if the future proved him wrong, he would still be ahead of the game, for the dog would be his best friend. And he wanted his dog to be a Beagle, the finest breed on earth, in the opinion of Art Purdy, and who knew more about dogs?

And what of his father's broken promise? Henry had stopped asking for a dog months before, convinced that his father couldn't afford to buy him one. Why else would he not keep his promise? His father had been hospitalized for a long time, and then there had been the cost of the new home and the moving expenses. Only recently he had over-heard his parents discussing the difficulties of getting a profitable law practice rolling in Green Valley. Henry could put two and two together.

So the boy had determined to find his own dog, his own Beagle. But where does one go to find a free Beagle? Now, on this late afternoon, his hopes were soaring.

"I have some writing I must do before dinner," he told his mother when he reached home.

"Go right ahead," Josie agreed. She thought it a bit odd that he was so anxious to tackle his homework on a Friday, with the whole weekend ahead, but she wasn't about to question his desire. Studies came before chores. Still, she made a mental note to have him bring in more logs for the fireplace after dinner.

Henry's writing was of a personal nature. A long overdue letter to Jerry Walker, his best friend back in the city:

> Sorry that I've taken so long to answer, [he began] but this country living keeps me hopping. There's always so much to do. As to things you asked about, the answer to going steady is 'no' so far, although I am becoming more interested in a girl named Bess, who is beautiful enough to make you stop raving about Grace. The fellows here are an odd bunch. I've had a few fights, but none recently. They

28

know they can't push me around. Yes, the teachers are tougher than where you are. And 'no,' I don't have my dog yet, but expect to get one shortly. I have decided to get a Beagle, but want a good one, and good ones are hard to find. Just heard of one that is really tops, and intend to see him as soon as possible. Mr. Purdy, a friend of mine here who is a famous dog authority, has been helping me in my search. I know you think I should get a Bedlington, because you have one, but I need a hunting dog. Yours is okay for the city just as a pet. How are you? I am fine. Will send you a picture of my dog soon.

At the service station, Art Purdy was trying to be even more helpful. Sam Hawthorne had dropped by for gas. He was in a hurry, but he was courteous enough to sit in his car for ten minutes and listen to Art's story about the city couple who had abandoned a pup at the lake.

"Who told you about this?" asked Sam when he had the chance.

"Nobody," said Art.

"Then how do you know?"

"I know because I'm a sound judge of character and the dog was not in their car," Art explained. "I'm telling you this because you may find the dog, and if so, I want you to give the dog to Henry Deane."

"Who?"

"Henry Deane, the new lawyer's son. Henry wants a Beagle, so don't send this one to the pound, okay?"

Sam agreed and drove off and thought no more about the Beagle. The last male descendant of one of Hudson Valley's oldest families, he worked for the town garage as a mechanic and supplemented his income as dog warden. The pay for the warden's job was inconsistent, and that was why nobody else wanted it. Sam was paid two dollars per head for every stray or unlicensed dog he delivered to the county dog pound. The rate for a stray cat was one dollar. Animals not claimed within ten days were destroyed, but that was not his responsibility.

Over the years, September and October had proved to be his most profitable months. They could have been even more lucrative, but Sam regarded the money as somewhat immoral. He had grown up on a farm and was both a nature and animal lover, and did not pursue his duties as warden too arduously. His wife was expecting a baby, and Sam figured he had a real excuse for not running around the countryside looking for stray dogs. He wanted to be home as much as possible.

His daughter Bess, aged thirteen, was taking wash off the line when he drove into his yard. "How is your mother?" he asked.

"She's fine," Bess told him. "She's ironing."

"Ironing? At a time like this?"

"For heaven's sake, Dad," laughed Bess. "The baby isn't due for three months."

"Ten weeks!" he said. Then he hurried into the house and told his wife Mary that she should be resting.

She agreed, but went right on ironing as she told him to answer two telephone calls—one from Peter and one from Mrs. Wilson.

He answered the calls in reverse order. From Mrs. Wilson who was famous for her kennel of Poodles, he learned that a strange dog had been seen on her grounds in recent days.

"I am sure that he is homeless and I wish you would capture him and take him away. You understand that I cannot

30

expose my dogs to disease carriers. This one is a big, black mongrel."

Sam promised to see what he could do. Then he called Sheriff Peter Long.

"Just wanted to let you know that a pack of dogs hit the pheasant pens at the game farm near Brewster last night," said Peter. "Killed about thirty cocks and I don't know how many hens. Must have been quite a commotion there, but nobody heard anything. It was raining, of course. From the tracks in the mud, I'd say that black devil King was back in these parts again. Hoped we'd heard the last of him. Oh, I know Brewster is twenty miles away, but that's just a stroll for a bad actor like King. So keep your eyes open when you're driving around, and be sure to pack a gun. Thanks for calling, Sam."

Mary asked about the phone calls during dinner and Sam told her about the news from Peter.

"I hope it is King," said Bess. "I mean, I hope he's still alive. He's such a brave dog."

Sam changed the subject by asking Bess how things had gone in school that day. So the mention of the big black mongrel did not occur again until after the Hawthornes had retired. It was a still night, and neither of them was very sleepy.

"You didn't approve of what Bess said about that dog King, did you?" asked Mary. "Sam? Did you hear me?"

"Oh, I heard you," he assured her. "I was thinking how to answer, and remembering what Bess said a couple of years ago about that dog. She said that the only thing wrong with him was that nobody had ever loved him, and that if she ever met him, why she'd kiss him on the nose and then he'd be a good boy."

"You sound angry."

"I'm not. I just don't want a kid of mine kissing any strange dog on the nose—especially that King. Maybe half the stories about him aren't true, but he's no better than a wild animal. And here's Bess, over thirteen now, and she's no different than the other kids in town. King is their hero or something. They think he's half Rin Tin Tin and half Robin Hood."

Mary laughed and said, "If I know our Bess, she was just leading up to something, and you didn't give her the chance to continue."

"Oh?"

"Her 4-H Club is planning a project in dog care and obedience, if enough children are interested. Bess is interested, but she'll need a dog of her own. We thought perhaps you could find a good one for her. You're always picking up homeless puppies."

"I'll keep an eye out for a good one." he promised.

"Thank you," she said, and then she was silent for a long time before she asked, "Sam? Are you awake?"

"Yes."

"If you went looking for King, and you found him, could you shoot him?"

He considered for a moment before replying, "I think so. Shooting pack-dogs is part of my job, isn't it?"

They were brave words, but she didn't think he meant them. Sam had never taken advantage of the county law—again at two dollars a head—that permitted him to shoot pack dogs. Sam hated just the thought of shooting any dog.

Mary said nothing. Then she heard Sam's steady breathing and remembered, too late, that she had not mentioned her plans for a picnic. She had promised Bess that some Sunday soon, while the weather was still pleasant, they would

32

picnic at the old Thompson farm. It was one of their favorite places, and they hadn't been there in over a year.

Art Purdy snapped off the television set, turned to his wife and said, "You know something? Sometimes I talk too much."

"Not tonight. You've hardly said a word all evening."

"I've been thinking. It was a strange day, in a way, and I had the best intentions in the world." Then he told her about his talk with Henry Deane, and about how excited the boy was at the prospect of finding a homeless Beagle, and about the conversation with Sam Hawthorne. "I was just trying to be helpful, you know. Then, just as I was getting ready to close, George Deane drove in for gas and oil."

"The new lawyer?"

"Yes. Henry's father." Even after a year in Green Valley, George Deane was still the *new* lawyer, and would be until another lawyer came along and opened an office. "Well, I started kidding him, asking if he was a dog hater or something, because his son doesn't have a dog, you know. I asked him if lawyers aren't supposed to like dogs, for instance. And do you want to know something?"

"Yes."

"He likes dogs! Not only that, but he's ordered a pup for his son. A Collie. The wrong breed, of course."

"Of course."

"Yes, the boy should have a Beagle. Still, from George's point of view, the Collie is a nice touch. He told me that his parents gave him a Collie on his fourteenth birthday, and his father's parents gave him a Collie on his fourteenth birthday, if you follow me. I guess this has been going on for as long as there have been Deanes. When a Deane boy is fourteen, his birthday present is always a Collie. It's family tradition, you see."

"I understand."

"So Henry will be very surprised on his birthday. Disappointed, too. He really wants a Beagle." Art shook his head and sighed, "Yes, sometimes I talk too much."

≈≋ ≈≋ FOUR ≈≋ ≈≋

MURPHY HAD NEVER BEEN happier. He adjusted quickly to the strange living schedule of his new friends, and found the nights as acceptable as the days. Nor did he fret when King left the barn for long stretches during the daylight hours, for Rover always stayed behind. So he was never really alone, and King always returned.

The Beagle had inherited the inquisitiveness of his breed and tried to follow King on one of his daylight sorties. But the big black dog turned and snarled and snapped at him and drove him back to the barn. Murphy was surprised and a little frightened, and he made no move to follow King when he trotted off. It did not happen again. There was a lesson for him in the snarl, and he understood it.

Of the three in the hideaway, Murphy was the youngest. His body was still growing, still developing, and he needed more rest than the others. And because he was still growing,

35

he required more food, even though he was the smallest. His elders saw that he had plenty to eat, but it was more by accident than design. They ate quickly and recklessly, scattering and forgetting lesser morsels—so there was always enough left over for Murphy, who dined last. The pack had its own caste system.

In number, King's pack was smaller than average: Himself, Rover, the part-time Sport, and the newcomer Murphy. It had been larger by four some months earlier, but the others had become careless—all in fatal fashion: One had been caught in the jaws of a trap; another had been tempted by poisoned meat; and two others had gorged themselves on the body of a lamb with such concentration that they did not sense the approach of the farmer who shot them.

Since early spring, King and his pack had been conducting their business far from the home base on the southern outskirts of Green Valley. The leader was quite willing to travel half the night or more, in the interest of survival. He found that two or three weekly forays were sufficient for the purpose. Between times, he and the pack relaxed at the old farm. The bleached bones of many victims, scattered about the weedy premises and the basement floor, attested the fact that they brought some of the larder home. And at the farm, between raids, they did not overlook the local supply of small wild animals and game birds, or an occasional fawn.

It was a good life and King was a wise leader. Indeed, about the time Murphy had joined them, King had decided to change his tactics. Influenced, perhaps, by the memory of his two comrades who had lingered too long, he concluded that things were getting too dangerous on the distant grounds. He had not operated in Green Valley for almost a

year, and the other packs in the county respected his territory. So it seemed time to favor the local scene with his pa-
tronage. For awhile, at least, the element of surprise would
be in his favor. While alert humans searched for his pack in
distant pastures, the pack would be reaping its harvest close
to home.

Of all the members of the pack, Rover understood King
best and thought his almost daily absences were in the nature of scouting trips. But this was not the real reason. An
instinct that King could not deny drew him to the Poodle
kennel, where a number of the bitches were in season. By
night, he had not been able to force entry to the kennel, so
he studied the situation from a little hill overlooking the kennel runs by day.

The hill was dotted with scrub pines and provided several excellent vantage points. He preferred a hidden position, so that the bitches below were not aware they were
being spied upon.

He had a clear view of the midday feeding operation.
First, the woman and the little girl appeared outside their
house, about two hundred feet from the kennel. The woman
always carried two buckets, and the little girl cradled a pile
of dog dishes in her arms. The two proceeded down the
slight slope to the kennel, where the dishes were placed on
a long bench and the food was spooned from buckets into
the dishes. During all of this activity the Poodles barked and
the woman shouted for quiet.

The big black dog may have wondered how food prepared
by loving hands would taste. Or he may have concluded that
if he couldn't share his love with any of the bitches, at least
he could demonstrate what a brave fellow they were miss-

ing. In any event, he devised a foolish, simple plan to sample the food. Foolish, because it would have to be conducted by day. Simple, because the woman and the little girl did not carry weapons.

He could have worked alone, but the pack habit was too strong within him, and this would be his chance to show Murphy a professional in action.

Rover and Murphy were troubled about their leader that night. They were more than a little hungry, but King continued to sleep. It was not like him.

Sport arrived about midnight. He sat down and waited for King to stir; and, when the black dog did not oblige, Sport stretched out and went to sleep, too; but he was well fed.

When Rover moved out of the basement, Murphy followed him. They trotted to the nearby stream to quench their thirst. Satisfied, the two started back for the barn. Murphy then scented the presence of a rabbit nearby. He stopped. The scent was tempting, surely, but something held him back.

Rover had also come to a stop. He turned and walked back to Murphy to see what delayed him. At that moment, the rabbit moved in the brush. It was an act of innocence; but Rover, with a mighty leap and crunching of jaws, made sure that it was also fatal.

Murphy did not immediately partake of the meal. But when he observed that no harm befell Rover, he tasted a rabbit leg and found it to his liking. Thus, he overcame his unnatural hesitancy and became a rabbit hunter, and true to his breed.

Their appetites somewhat appeased, they returned to the hideaway and joined the two others in sleep.

About dawn, Sport got up, stretched and trotted off for his woodshed. As far as he was concerned, it had been a lost night.

The other three slept on until King stirred about mid-day. They visited the stream, where King lapped water leisurely while Murphy and Rover watched. Then King jumped the stream and paused just long enough to turn his head as if to signal the other two.

Rover jumped the stream and Murphy waded it. They followed King through the field and into the woods. All the way to the Poodle kennel, the pack kept to the woods.

The dogs didn't know it was Sunday, but Sally Wilson did. Her daddy was home. He was a traveling salesman and was only home on Sundays, except for vacations.

Sally was the daughter of William and Dorothy Wilson, owners of Willdo Kennel, a name well-known in Standard Poodle circles. She was very serious about dogs, but not nearly as serious or knowledgeable as her mother. And Sally was proud to be permitted to help her mother care for the Poodles.

William was still asleep when Sally and her mother left the house to feed the Poodles. As usual, the Poodles in the kennel barked up a clamorous din as soon as they saw their dinners approaching. The woman shouted to them to be quiet, but they paid no attention; they probably didn't hear her. Some just sat and barked; some ran around and barked; a few jumped straight up and down—all four feet off the ground, and barked.

King and Rover and Murphy were watching from their stations on the hill. The leader was waiting until the woman reached the halfway point to the kennel before putting his plan into action.

Murphy didn't know what he was doing there, or what the plan of action was, but he did know that the smallest human figure was a child. He had played with children at the lake several times during the summer and had really enjoyed himself. Youth's attraction for youth is very strong. Even wild bear cubs have been known to frolic in harmless fashion with children.

Now, to the utter dismay of King, the Beagle broke from ambush and ran toward the child. He yipped with joy as he ran, but the continuing din from the Poodles smothered the sounds. Sally pointed to the onrushing Murphy. "Look, Mama," she cried. "A little dog!"

At the same moment, King and Rover sprang from their hiding places and raced for Sally and Mrs. Wilson. Their long legs carried them past Murphy who was still fifty feet from the little girl.

The woman stood very still. She did not like the looks of the strange dogs. Suddenly, her surprise turned to fear and then to panic. "Run for the house!" she cried, and the little girl obeyed.

Just as the woman turned to run, she stumbled and fell, and the two buckets flew from her hands. She did not attempt to rise; the fall had restored her power of reason, and she knew it would be safer to lie still and play dead.

King reached her first. He circled her and sniffed and knew she was alive. He glanced around and saw twenty quarts of mixed dog food on the ground. He stepped over to a mound of food and sampled a mixture of ground beef, kibble, cod liver oil and powdered vitamins for the first time in his life—he found it flavorsome and so did Rover. They ate unhurriedly, keeping alert eyes on the woman, who did not move. Overall, it was a quiet scene, for as soon as the woman had fallen, the puzzled Poodles had stopped their barking.

Murphy, meanwhile, had followed the little girl and even tried to be friendly, but she threw the dog dishes at him and slammed the door in his face. He waited a few moments outside the door, then returned to his friends to claim his share of the delicious food that still remained.

In the house, the little girl awakened her daddy and sobbed out her story. He dashed to the window and saw the three strange dogs hovering over his wife. He rushed to a closet for his shotgun, but could not locate any shells. Downstairs, he found his .22 rifle and again he hunted for ammunition. There were only three bullets in a kitchen drawer. He loaded the rifle and ran out of the house, shooting at the dogs as he ran. The first two shots went wild, and the third buried into the ground, inches from his wife's head. The dogs were never really in danger.

He shot as rapidly as he could, but King was off and running before the trigger was pressed a second time. The black dog never saw the man, but he knew the dangerous sound of a rifle.

Murphy hightailed after him. Only Rover was confused. He fled in the opposite direction, straight for the man. Escape was on Rover's mind, but the man did not know that. William Wilson climbed the nearest tree. His wife continued playing possum.

By then, the little girl had regained her composure to the extent that she remembered how dangerous moments were handled on television. She picked up the phone, dialed the operator and said, "Please listen carefully. We need help. Inform the Federal Bureau of Investigation." She hung up the phone and went to the window and looked out. Then she laughed. In all her seven years, she had never before seen her daddy up a tree.

Sam Hawthorne and his family arrived at the old Thompson farm about noon. They parked the car on the dirt road and walked up the path—really only traces of a path that had once led directly to the front door of the farmhouse; only the crumbling foundation and the stone doorstep remained. Sam pointed out the numerals etched in the stone and explained—as he had on previous visits—the house had been built in 1898. "And look there, Bess. That used to be the cellar. Now it looks like a nursery for maple saplings, wouldn't you say?"

They spread a blanket on level ground near two ancient, dying apple trees, and as Mary and Bess unpacked the picnic basket and arranged things, Sam guessed aloud that the trees were probably Baldwins. "You might think, since they haven't been bearing apples for many years, that they'd served their purpose in life. Well, the woodpeckers still find them handy for meals, and I'll bet if we came up here in June, we'd find bluebirds nesting."

Mary smiled. She knew how Sam loved to impart such gems of nature to Bess, and she was glad that he had agreed to come on the picnic. He had been a bit moody in recent days, and now he seemed to be enjoying himself.

After lunch, Mary propped herself against a tree and read the Sunday papers, while Sam and Bess strolled around the farm. They found a walled spring, choked with leaves, where the farmer's wife had filled her pails a half century before. Then they circled fields where cows had once grazed, and finally they came to the remnants of the old barn. "They probably kept a wagon and a carriage down below there," said Sam. "Or maybe pigs. My grandfather used to keep pigs under his barn."

"Let's go down," suggested Bess. "We might find some old tools or something."

"Don't try it," Sam told her. "If one of those rotted beams gives way, you'll never know what hit you."

"Then let's go back to the stream. I want to look for arrowheads."

"You go ahead. I feel more like a nap," Sam suggested. He went back to Mary and explained where Bess had gone and added, "She gets prettier every day, but she'll never be as pretty as you." Then he folded the blanket into a pillow and stretched out on the ground.

No one saw or heard the richly fed King, Rover or Murphy when they returned. The trio had approached the farm through the woods and had been watching the people from a distance. Indeed, Murphy, who had lain down to rest, was already asleep.

While Murphy slept, King and Rover exchanged looks and reached silent agreement. The big black dog moved to the fringe of the woods to keep a closer watch on the big people. Rover stayed with Murphy and watched Bess as she explored the near bank of the stream.

The girl was almost out of sight and Rover was ready to change position. Then, the unexpected happened. Bess, attempting to cross the stream, lost her footing on a rock and sat down in the cold water. The sound of her laughter penetrated Murphy's sleep. His tail wagged and his feet twitched, and his jaws emitted little grunts of pleasure. Rover attempted to quiet him with nuzzling, but that only awakened the dreaming Beagle. It took a few moments for the little hound to realize that he was hearing real laughter and not dream-laughter. And then he forgot that he was supposed to stay in hiding. King was not there to curl his lips back in warning.

For the second time that day, the call of youth to youth was too strong for Murphy. He jumped up, barked, and ran off to join the laughing girl. Rover retreated into the woods and worked his way toward King. As far as the yellow dog was concerned, Murphy was a helpless amateur.

By the time Mary arrived on the scene to investigate her daughter's shrieks of laughter, Murphy was retrieving sticks thrown into the stream by Bess, and both he and the girl were soaking wet. "Where on earth did he come from?" asked Mary.

"I don't know, he just appeared after I fell into the water. He's very friendly."

Murphy was a little shy with Mary, but she didn't force her friendship upon him, and he accepted her within minutes. Her touch was gentle when she petted him, and he licked her hand as a sign of total acceptance.

It didn't take too long for the distaff side of the family to convince Sam that the Beagle pup would make a good pet for Bess. He agreed, but his terms were conditional: "We're assuming that the dog doesn't have a home. But he looks like a pretty good Beagle to me, and chances are he has an owner somewhere. So we'll only keep him if we can't find his owner."

"Then let's take him home right now," said Mary. "If

Bess doesn't get out of those wet clothes, she'll catch pneumonia."

So Murphy accompanied the Hawthornes when they drove home, and King and Rover watched his departure. Murphy's friends would sleep in the woods that night. The black dog felt uneasy about the hideaway.

And the boy named Henry Deane watched, too. He was just coming around the last bend in the narrow dirt road, when the Hawthornes started for home. The boy had to step aside as the car passed him, and he had a close view of his Beagle sitting on Bess Hawthorne's lap.

He stood there and watched the car until it disappeared. He was sure that the dog warden would turn his Beagle over to the pound, and there was nothing that he could do to prevent it. In that moment, the boy's hopes and dreams were shattered. He felt hollow inside.

Then he remembered that there was one thing he wanted to do—if not for the Beagle, for the Beagle's friends. The paper bag in his hip pocket contained three lamb chops, secretly borrowed from his mother's freezer.

The boy walked down the road to the old Thompson farm. He placed the three lamb chops side by side on the stone doorstep of the house that was no longer there. Then he started the long walk home. A few hours before, he had traveled the same route with a smile on his face and many happy dreams to shorten the miles. This time he walked slowly, and his face reflected despair.

FIVE

"WASN'T THAT THE DEANE boy?" asked Mary Hawthorne. She waited for an answer from her daughter, who sat on the rear seat with the dog in her lap. "Did you hear me, Bess?"

"Sorry. What did you say?"

Mary turned and looked at Bess. "The boy we just passed. Wasn't that Henry Deane?"

"Yes."

"You're blushing."

"I am not!"

Then silence prevailed until Sam said, "The boy spends a lot of time at Art's gas station. What's he like, Bess?"

"Well, I hardly know him, really. I mean, we sit next to each other in algebra, and I have danced with him at the school dances. The girls think he's cute. Sally and Eloise think he has a crush on me. I wouldn't know. I mean—oh, you know what I mean."

"What?" asked her father.

"Now, Sam!" said Mary.

"But I don't know what she means. The boy dances, we learned that. But there must be more to him than that. For instance, is he smart? Or does he want to be a lawyer like his father?"

"He wants to be a veterinarian, I think," said Bess, still blushing. "Look, Mom, did you see this, on our dog's right leg?"

"I did, but don't worry. It's healing nicely."

"I noticed it and it's not deep," Sam commented. "I'd say he got too close to a car, except that he doesn't seem to be car-shy."

Murphy sensed they were talking about him and he licked Bess' face. He was sitting on her lap and enjoying the ride. When he wasn't licking her face and hands he was sticking his head out the window to view the countryside; he was quiet for no more than two or three seconds at a time.

Once home, they brought him into the house where he spent a busy few hours sniffing strange new scents and exploring things. It didn't bother him, and he didn't beg, when the humans supped. He was the last to be served in the pack, and he was used to waiting for his turn. After the family supper hour, he dined in magnificent fashion—for the second time that day—on tasty table scraps, a bowl of milk and several lumps of sugar.

"He has manners," Sam observed, "and that means somebody trained him. He's used to seeing people eating, and knows that he shouldn't beg. So I'm afraid he has an owner somewhere."

"I don't think so, because he doesn't have a special name," said Bess. "He responds to whatever name I call him."

48

"Let's give him a name," Mary suggested.

But Sam objected, pointing out that a new name wouldn't be fair to the dog, for it would only confuse him if he already had a name and went back to his owner. "And we don't know if he's used to sleeping in a house, or even if he's housebroken," Sam continued. "So I think, until we're sure that we can keep him, that he'll stay in the garage at night. I'll fix a nice bed for him there."

He made a dog bed out of an old cardboard carton, and he lined it with straw. Then he found a chain collar that fit the puppy just right. Not too tight. After Bess said goodnight and had gone to bed, Sam carried Murphy to the garage and placed him on the straw. Finally, he rummaged around on his work bench until he found a ten-foot length of light chain. He attached one end of it to the bumper of his car, and the other end to Murphy's collar. He patted Murphy and wished him a good night's sleep and left. Out of habit, he almost closed the garage doors tight. But he remembered that the puppy would need fresh air, and left the doors ajar.

Murphy remained in his bed until he heard the door of the house shut. Then he stepped to the car and sniffed at the metal body and under it found one of the sources of the strange, unappetizing scent of gasoline and oil. Then he started toward the garage doors, but the chain held him back. He tried walking in the other direction, and the same thing happened. It was his first experience with restraint of this nature, and he didn't know how to cope with it.

He sat down and tried to scratch the collar off his neck, alternating his hind feet. The effort was to no avail, so he lay down on his stomach and tried to pry the collar away with his front paws—again with no success. He was puzzled, but not for long. The chain held him back whenever he went away from the bed, but when he walked toward it, the chain dragged on the floor. So he retired to his bed and lay down and sure enough, it was simple to work the slack of the chain between his jaws. He was determined to bite through it, for he was alone again, and he didn't like that feeling.

He had just started to chew on the chain when the garage doors creaked open and Sam returned. Sam was bringing a pan of water for Murphy, but he didn't bother to turn on a light. He merely placed the pan next to the bed, patted Murphy, and departed—and again he left the doors slightly ajar.

"The pup settled right down," Sam reported to Mary. "He likes his bed. We won't be troubled by any howling tonight, that's for sure."

Even as Sam spoke, Murphy renewed his efforts to chew through the chain, but he didn't devote too much time to the task. He soon realized that he was not making any progress, and the links hurt his teeth when he clamped down with real pressure.

He was tired and well fed anyway, and those combined conditions made him sleepy. So he closed his eyes and went to sleep for a few hours.

He was awakened by the eerie baying of a Coonhound in the far distance. He started for the doors to investigate and only remembered the length of chain when it brought him to an abrupt halt. Now the thing really irritated him. He started to fight it, pulling against it with all his might, twisting and turning his head and body until, quite accidentally, his back was to the doors. He felt the collar slip a little over one ear. As he crouched and backed away, he shook his head. Suddenly the straining chain pulled the collar over both ears. Murphy was free!

The sudden release sent him tumbling against one of the doors, and it opened a few inches more. He scrambled to his feet and escaped from the garage. Then he ran as fast as he could.

Murphy liked the Hawthornes and his stay with them was enjoyable, but he had no way of knowing that they intended to make a home for him. However, he did know that they had left him alone, and he did not like being left alone.

So Murphy ran through the remainder of the night. He knew where he was running and why: Back to the hideaway and his friends.

But he did not know where the old farm was.

Bess was dressed an hour earlier than usual. She was anxious to play with the Beagle before breakfast. She had hardly closed the door of the house behind her when she opened it again and rushed back in to shout the terrible news: The Beagle had escaped!

It was a sad morning for the Hawthorne family. Bess cried and didn't eat a thing for breakfast and she didn't want to go to school—but she did. Her mother blamed herself for agreeing to take the puppy home; her father regretted his own carelessness—the collar seemed to fit properly, but obviously it hadn't.

Before he left for work that morning, Sam promised Mary that he would do his best to find the dog. As a first step, he stopped at the service station to talk to Art Purdy. If anyone found a Beagle, Art would hear the news sooner or later.

Come to think of it, the pup might have been one of Art's.

"One of your pups missing, by any chance, Art?" asked Sam as he walked into the tiny office. Only then did he notice that Sheriff Peter Long was sitting there, half hidden by the file cabinet.

"I asked him the same thing ten minutes ago and the answer is no," said Peter. "What do you think about this thing, Sam?"

"What thing?"

"You know, the doings over at the Poodle kennel yesterday."

"Sorry, Peter. I don't know what you're talking about," said Sam. He looked to Art for an explanation, and Art handed him a copy of the *Times*.

"Where you been, in outer space?" asked Art. "Page 28, third column."

Sam had no trouble finding the story under the headline WILD DOGS THREATEN FAMILY. It wasn't a long story—two hundred words or so—and he read it twice, because he found it hard to believe. Then he tossed the newspaper on the desk and sat down and thought about what he had read. He had never heard of a pack acting that way—actually attacking human beings—nor had millions of others who read the same story that morning, and most of them were surprised to learn that pack dogs existed in the midst of civilization.

The other two men sat and waited for Sam's comment, and when it came it was, "Well I'll be damned! First I've heard of it. Must have happened about the time we started on the picnic. Didn't talk to anyone last night. Nobody phoned me."

"They sure phoned me," said Peter. "People are calling me all sorts of names for permitting pack-dogs to run loose in Green Valley. You'd think I raised the dogs and personally trained them to attack the Wilson family."

"You think it's the same pack that hit the game farm at Brewster?" asked Sam.

Peter nodded. "Looks that way," he said. "Eight or ten dogs. The Wilsons weren't sure, it all happened so fast. And we can be positive about one thing: King is back. Mrs. Wilson got a close look at him. A big black dog with only one ear."

"Don't be so sure," advised Art. "If you ask me, the woman was hysterical and doesn't remember what she saw. Who ever heard of a Beagle in a pack? Ridiculous!"

"Sorry to disillusion you, Art, but this time it's a fact," said Peter. "I had a long talk with Mrs. Wilson. All three of the Wilsons got a good look at the hound, and he nearly tore the door down trying to get at the little girl. Why, they were so close to him that they all saw a sore or a wound high on his right thigh."

Art shook his head and said, "There has never been a mean Beagle! This woman is trying to ruin the breed's reputation and boost the Poodle's. I'm tempted to write the President and tell him not to believe everything he reads in the newspapers."

The others didn't laugh. Art wasn't even sure that they had heard him. No one said anything for a minute, and then Sam coughed and acted like he was about to say something, but he didn't.

Finally the sheriff broke the silence. He stood up and said, "Well, we'll have to do something, Sam, and I suppose it

53

will be the same as always. Pray for luck that we spot the pack. Maybe we can knock off two or three and scare the rest out of the township. Trouble is, this shapes up as one of those wide-ranging packs, and not even the Lord knows where the dogs will hit next." He went to the door, paused then turned and said, "When you find the time, Sam, look around the old iron mines, and pack a gun. We found King's tracks around the iron dumps a couple of years ago, remember?" He waved and left the office.

"Now there goes a confused man," said Art. "I know Beagles and the Poodle lady doesn't, but he accepts her word. What do you think, Sam?"

"I'm confused, too, and I'm late for work. See you later, Art."

And Sam was confused. He was also tempted to tell the others about the dog he'd found at the old Thompson farm, but he didn't and he wondered why. He found it hard to believe that his hound and the pack hound were one and the same—but was the sore on the thigh just a coincidence? Could a killer dog turn into a loving dog in the space of a few hours? Sam didn't think so.

Still, just on the chance that he was wrong, he thought he'd check the old Thompson farm when he had the time. The pack had to be hiding somewhere. He'd check there first, since it was closer, and leave the iron mines until later.

Henry could hardly wait for algebra class that day. He was no longer sure that the dog warden would turn the Beagle over to the pound. What if Sam Hawthorne kept the dog for himself?

54

The boy was in his seat early, and as soon as Bess Hawthorne sat down next to him, he told her about seeing the Beagle on her lap the day before.

"Yes," she said, "we found him at the old Thompson farm." And then she started to cry.

Her tears increased his anxiety. Had something happened to his Beagle? An accident? Had he run off and been hit by a car? Had they taken him to the pound and shot him already? Could they do a thing like that?

Then the class bell rang and Bess managed to compose herself. She said, very quickly, "I'm sorry, it's just that we wanted to keep him, but he ran away during the night, and my father promised to look for him. I'll tell you about it later."

She did just that when class was over, and Henry told her how sorry he was, too. He hoped that he sounded sincere, but he wasn't sorry—he was relieved and happy and full of dreams again. His dog could belong only to him, and he was willing to believe that the Beagle—in some mysterious fashion—was aware of this and had run away to find Henry Deane. It was pure fantasy, and he recognized it as such, but it was pleasant to muse about and finally it led to thoughts about mental telepathy. Was it possible? He would ask Art Purdy.

So after school Henry visited Art and asked, "Do you believe in mental telepathy?"

Art scratched his head, pursed his lips, and said, "Yes and no. At times I lean to the physical. Why?"

"I was wondering if dogs could have mental telepathy?"

"Yes," said Art, the man who knew all there was to know about dogs, by his own admission, "or maybe I should say yes and no, because some breeds have it and some don't."

"Do Beagles have it?"

"Yes. The breed is at the head of the list. I'd say the average Beagle pup starts developing it at around six months, more or less." Then a customer drove in for gas and Art was happy to serve him. The boy's questions were getting a bit complex.

Henry started to walk home. Along the way his thoughts were concentrated on the Beagle. If the Beagle were concentrating on him, their paths would cross sooner or later. The boy was not entirely sold on mental telepathy, but it would do no harm to try. It was the sort of dreaming that might come true. If he had known how to go about it, or if Art had been able to advise him, he would have tried his hand at working a miracle, too.

The boy knew what had happened the day before at Willdo Kennel, and that there had been a Beagle in the pack. But it didn't worry him, for he knew that his Beagle was above that sort of thing, and that his Beagle had been at the old farm anyway.

Was the Beagle a Jekyll and Hyde? Sam hoped that he wouldn't find out as he drove to the old Thompson farm right after breakfast on Saturday morning. He hadn't discussed that question with his family during the week, and he hadn't told his wife or his daughter where he was going that morning. They assumed he had some extra work to do at the town garage.

He parked his car on the side of the dirt road some distance from the farm, loaded his shotgun and pushed on the safety. Then he walked through the woods until he reached the stream, and from there he proceeded upstream to the point where Bess had fallen into the water.

That's when Sam almost turned back. For days, he was certain that he would shoot the pack dogs if he found them, but now he wasn't so sure that he could go through with it. Finally, he made a decision: He would shoot any and all pack dogs he found except the Beagle. Mary and Bess would never forgive him if he shot the little hound. They didn't have to know, of course, but he couldn't forgive himself for such an act. He was in complete agreement with Art Purdy. Mrs. Wilson had to be wrong. If a Beagle did run with the pack, then his role was nothing more than a mascot.

Now Sam felt better about his private mission. He worked his way very slowly upstream, alert for tracks along both banks and pausing now and then to study the weeds and the brush. He was looking for approach paths as well as tracks, for even wild dogs must drink. One he was startled by the sudden flight of a kingfisher from a branch overhanging the stream. Moments later, he nearly fell into the water as a grouse thundered away almost from under his feet. That was when he thought he saw something moving through the woods, but he couldn't be sure. His imagination was playing tricks on him; he had the feeling that he was being watched, and he shivered at the thought. He pushed off the safety on the shotgun, and proceeded upstream.

He found what he was looking for a hundred yards away: Dog tracks not more than a day old. Two dogs at least, maybe more. The imprint of one canine paw was the biggest he had ever seen. Sam was relieved to note that none of the tracks were small.

Five minutes later, he discovered another drinking place.

The tracks were not fresh, but the big paws were there again. Now he knew that the dogs who made the tracks were frequent visitors to the area. Pack dogs? Yes, and here were the prints of a small dog, round and compact. They were off to one side and he had almost missed them.

His certainty was destroyed almost immediately. Looking down between his feet, he saw the imprint of a boy's left shoe. Well, maybe it was a man's shoe. Then he found other imprints, rights and lefts, all for the same size shoe. Again he was unable to judge the age of the prints, but it looked like a person had accompanied the dogs. Perhaps he was the owner of the dogs. He compared the size and depth with the imprints of his own shoes and reckoned that the other person was smaller and weighed about one-ten. The owner may have been a boy.

Sam left the stream and crossed a field to the old farm. On the way, he found a path through the overgrowth that had been made by some animal or animals. It was just a slight path, and it could have been made by dogs or deer. He followed it a short distance and decided that it headed in the direction of what had once been a barn.

He approached the old barn site cautiously. When he reached a point where he had a good view of the basement, he stopped. Then, quite by accident, he discovered something that resembled a piece of old bone. With one foot, he pushed the dead grass and leaves away, and found that it was more than just a small piece. It had once been the thigh of a lamb or a kid.

He looked for more bones and they were not difficult to find. He thought, there's everything here except dinosaur and ostrich. At the entrance to the barn basement, he also found an old dried chicken wing, with some feathers still attached—Barred Rock. He couldn't recall anyone around Green Valley with a flock of Barred Rocks.

Sam stepped into the old basement, first checking to make sure that the beam overhead was not rotted. Half hidden among the debris of old leaves, sticks, and pieces of wood on the dirt floor was even more evidence of past meals. He wondered how he had missed seeing some of it when he had pointed out the place to Bess.

He thought he heard a noise coming from the direction of the corner, where fallen beams and caved-in flooring had formed a shelter. It was less than twenty feet away. He stood there holding his breath. It was not a solid shelter by any means, and there were only two places a man could walk through. He thought he saw a moving shadow on the foundation wall. Then he was sure, for a second shadow moved, but he heard no sound.

Slowly, quietly, he brought the shotgun to his shoulder. He sighted once to the right and then to the left. That would do it, he thought. At such a short distance, two blasts would rip the entire area.

He fired both barrels, then quickly ejected the shells, reloaded, and brought the shotgun to the ready. He waited for more than a minute, but he heard nothing and he saw nothing.

With the gun still at his shoulder, Sam stepped to one of the openings and peered inside the semi-sheltered area. He could see every foot of it. It was empty.

Sam felt like a fool.

He didn't go near the doorstep, but even if he had he probably wouldn't have noticed the light blood stains on it. Henry's lamb chops were gone—they had made a fine, midnight snack for Sport, the sheriff's Setter. The part-time pack dog had been disappointed to find the black leader and the others missing from the hideout. He'd wolfed down the meat, slept a few hours, then trotted home before sunup. The sheriff fed him two hours later, and the dog had no difficulty consuming his second meal. When his master drove off to work, Sport went back to bed.

After Murphy had been taken away by the Hawthorne family, King and Rover did not use the hideaway. But the two dogs remained close enough to spy on it, and they wondered if the humans would come back again. They roamed the nearby woods most of the time and slept there, too. The sites they picked for sleeping were no more uncomfortable than the hideaway. They left the woods a few times but only to satisfy their hunger, and only then at a distance of miles from the farm. Their menu was thus limited to pheasant, rabbits, field mice and frogs.

The two dogs were a half a mile away when Sam visited the farm that morning. They were curled up, bodies pressed back to back, on the windless side of a sheltering rock, sleeping soundly. Old, soft pine needles provided their bedding.

Rover was the first to awaken. He felt thirsty. He stood up and yawned and shook his whole body to free the needles from his coat. Then he looked at King. The black dog opened one eye, and closed it. He wanted more sleep.

So Rover trotted off to the stream alone, not particularly alert to the world around him until he heard the rattling call of a kingfisher ahead of him. The yellow dog stopped and listened. He heard another sound in the brush and, with the utmost caution, he proceeded to investigate. He saw a man bending over something at the edge of the stream.

The dog continued to watch until the man walked upstream and out of sight. Rover returned to his leader and, by means of a magical communication that mortals cannot understand, related what he had seen.

The two dogs looked at each other, then hurried off in the direction of the man. So Sam had been under surveillance before he fired the shots.

At the first sound of gunfire, King turned his back on Sam and ran off into the woods, with Rover a few paces behind. They were closing a chapter of their lives without ceremony.

The black dog and the yellow dog never returned to their favorite hideaway. The canine mind does not concern itself with what might have been.

The dogs were professionals, and what they had seen and heard in the last few days had not spoken in their favor. Why, their trusting, foolish little sidekick had been abducted in front of their eyes! The mood of the territory had changed and it was no longer to their liking—guns had sounded twice. And so they moved along without regrets. Rover thought it was high time to do so. He would have preferred an earlier departure, but it had taken King a long time to make up his mind. Perhaps he waited as long as he did in the hope that Murphy would escape his captors and return.

The black dog didn't know that Murphy had escaped and was already searching for the old barn hideout. He had been fed well before his flight from the Hawthorne place, and food was not on his mind. He proceeded with great anticipation. It never occurred to him that he might not find the hideout and King.

The young hound trotted along for hours pausing now and again to quench his thirst at ponds and streams, avoiding homes and busy roads as much as possible—more out of habit than fear, for King had set an excellent example. Once in the late afternoon, his keen Beagle nose picked up the scent of a solitary canine in the same field of winter oats that he had crossed earlier. The scent was stronger on the grass than on the ground, and Murphy continued to follow the trail, but he never saw the stranger. It was sheer luck that prompted him to turn aside, for the stranger he was following was none other than himself. The Beagle had made a complete circle.

By sundown, he was miles from Green Valley, and his short legs were beginning to feel the strain. Still he pressed on, for he was following a most interesting path that wound its way upward between huge boulders and little clumps of scrub pines. The breeze against his face carried the promise of water, a promise so strong that Murphy wondered if he was approaching the lake he knew so well. The path seemed endless, and when it ended the pup found himself in a strange world of little lakes. He was in iron-mine country— open pit mines that had served America well during the war with England, but unused and flooded for almost two centuries. The waters were deep, sixty to a hundred feet.

Murphy explored each little lake. He had a refreshing swim in mind, but the water level in each was too far from the rims of the solid, rock banks. The pup looked for a way down to the water, but he didn't find it. He thought of jumping, but something told him not to. It was an instinct, a something common to all forms of life, that warned him of danger.

If Murphy had jumped, he would have enjoyed his swim, but later, he would have discovered that the water was a prison. He never would have found a way to get back to dry ground. It was a difficult feat for a grown man and impossible for a pup.

Now the Beagle returned to the path and started down it. Along the way, he found a rotted tree trunk and slept in its hollow for a few hours. It was night, and he was weary. He was also lucky, but he didn't know that.

People rarely visited the iron-mine country anymore. That was the reason King had staked out a claim there two years before.

❧❧ ❧❧ SIX ❧❧ ❧❧

WHEN GEORGE DEANE CAME back to the dinner table, his wife Josie uttered a complaint: "Why do people have to telephone you at this hour? Why can't they go to your office during the day? Aren't lawyers supposed to eat? Your coffee is cold. Henry, get your father a fresh cup. Who was it this time?"

"Dorothy Wilson."

"Who?"

"The woman who owns Willdo Kennel," Henry explained. "Poodles. She had that trouble with the pack dogs."

"Oh. What did she want, George? Was it important enough to interrupt our dinner?"

"What she wants, she's not going to get," George announced. "Somebody told her that she has every right to sue because of the pack dog business, and she wants me to handle the case. Ridiculous."

65

"Why?" asked Josie.

"Well, who can she sue? The pack dogs?"

"What about the people who owned the dogs when they were pets?" asked Henry. "Mr. Purdy says that people are responsible for pack dogs."

"He has a point," George admitted. "By the way, Henry, Art Purdy told me to tell you that he's writing to the President, telling him not to believe the story about a Beagle being in that pack."

Henry grinned and said, "You know something? I'll bet he does write the President. He's very serious about the Beagle breed."

The phone rang just then and Josie said, "I'll answer. If it's somebody who wants to talk to a lawyer, that somebody can wait until the lawyer's office hours tomorrow."

The telephone was in the next room, so neither husband nor son saw the look on her face when she discovered the caller was a girl who wanted Henry. "You want Henry?" she asked, her voice registering complete surprise.

"Yes," came the sweet, unaffected voice of the young girl. "Henry Deane. Isn't this his home?"

"One moment, please, I'll call him," Josie replied. Without thinking, she patted her hair, smoothed her blouse and centered the seam of her skirt. Then she walked to the door and said, "For you, Henry." She heard the tiny quaver in her voice, and hoped the others hadn't noticed. "A young lady."

"Really? Then excuse me," said Henry. He almost dashed from the room.

Josie closed the door behind him, then walked to the dinner table and sat down. She didn't look at George. She

66

felt silly, almost giddy, and was afraid that she was going to cry.

George studied his wife's face for a few moments before inquiring, "Is something wrong, Josie?"

"No."

"You act as if something is."

"It's a girl," she whispered. "Don't you understand? This is the first time a girl has ever telephoned Henry." Then her eyes filled with tears. "Oh, George. He's growing up! I'm so happy!"

"Well, make up your mind. If you're happy, then laugh."

"Don't you see, don't you understand? I'm so relieved. Here I was so worried about his being withdrawn, and all the while he's just been passing through a phase, just beginning to grow up."

"Of course. Just what I've been telling you right along. Henry is a true Deane. Although this is a bit premature. I think I started noticing girls when I was sixteen. Of course, times change. Things move faster these days."

Josie dabbed at her eyes with a napkin and said, "I just had to cry a little. To a mother, this is an historical moment."

Then Henry returned. He sat down at the table and casually finished his glass of milk while both his parents stared at him. He put his glass down, looked from one to the other, then asked, "Something wrong?"

"Not in here," said George, "but the way you dashed out of here, it seemed as though you expected an important message. Is everything all right?"

"Yes, but then that depends upon one's point of view," Henry explained. "The call was from Bess. She's in my algebra class."

"I'll bet she's pretty," said Josie.

Henry shrugged and continued, "She just wanted to tell me that her father didn't find the dog today. You see, they found a puppy on Sunday, but it ran away and now they can't find it."

"Bess?" asked Josie. "Bess who?"

"Bess Hawthorne."

"Well, a woman of distinction," George told them. "The Hawthornes have lived here for generations."

"She sounds like a very nice girl," Josie decided. "Where did you meet her?"

"In algebra," said Henry. "May I be excused, Dad? I have some homework." He whistled his way up the stairs to his room, where his homework consisted of drawing a box-trap to scale. Mental telepathy was all right, but he wanted to be practical too. Sooner or later, he'd track down the Beagle, and he wanted to be ready.

His parents lingered over their after-dinner coffee much longer than usual. Since school had started again, both of them had noticed a change in Henry and each had waited for the other to mention it first. Now, thanks to a telephone call from a young lady, each felt that the time was just right for an exchange of views.

In George Deane's opinion, there was nothing wrong with his son and there never had been. The boy was healthy, bright and respectful toward his elders, and who could ask for anything more? Henry was reserved, and sometimes too withdrawn, perhaps, and he had never been the most popular boy in his circle, but what was wrong with that? Not a thing! All boys are not cast from the same mold: Some are students and some are not; some are good and some are delinquents;

some are popular and some are independent; some are loud and others serene; but each develops and matures at his own rate. "The great men of today were not all live wires in their youth," George had often reminded his wife. "As a matter of fact, some were so dull that their mothers worried themselves into early graves." This remark usually brought conversations about Henry to an end, for Josie could anticipate George's next sally, "My dear, I wish you wouldn't subscribe to so many magazines. The advice-to-parents articles are written by people who have never been parents, or by women who hate children, or by men who never were children."

Josie had never found a way to really penetrate her husband's paternal armor. George was not a demonstrative man, indeed he was sometimes close to being stuffy, and it was impossible for her to enlist his support when she admitted her worries about Henry. For she did worry. Her son was quite unlike any boy she could remember from her own youth, and he was certainly the opposite of young George Deane, if family scrapbooks were honest. George had been quite an athlete, for one thing, and Henry wasn't at all interested in sports. In the city, his chief interest had been to own a dog, mostly because Jerry Walker owned one, and she hadn't even heard him talking about that in recent months. Would the birthday Collie, still two months away, put some spirit into Henry, excite him, open up all sorts of doors to other interests and friends? She hoped so, and she was happy that George, who had so much on his mind—his health, and his new practice in Green Valley, to name two—had not forgotten the Deane family tradition.

"Speaking of the young lady's phone call," said George

on this night, "it doesn't surprise me at all. I think Henry has finally found himself. He's certainly showing more of the Deane character of late."

"I've noticed. He seems much happier since school began again."

"I'll admit I was a little worried about him."

"Oh?"

"The dog business, you know. I was almost sure that he resented me because I hadn't kept my promise. I almost told him about the Collie that was coming."

"Why don't you tell him now?"

The lawyer thought about it, then shook his head and said, "No, he's finding himself and it's best this way. I want him to be surprised." He looked at her for a long moment, smiled and asked, "Josie? Not worried about him any more?"

"I'll always worry," she said. "That's what mothers are for. And you should worry, too. At this rate, Henry will never become a football star."

She was teasing, but he misunderstood and replied, "Dartmouth is proud of its scholars, too."

They didn't understand the change in Henry. The new Henry was based on the boy's own determination. One day he would learn that determination isn't enough, not even when it's supported by strong hopes and dreams. Chance must be there, too—and you don't go out to find chance, it finds you.

"Anything new?" whispered Henry in algebra class the next day.

Bess shook her head and whispered back, "My father

doesn't have much time to look for him. Would you help me look, Henry? Please?"

He was a gentleman, and he nodded, but he deliberately refrained from uttering the word *yes*. The boy was determined to find the Beagle—or to trap him, which amounted to the same thing—but for himself, not for Bess Hawthorne or anyone else. For the rest of the school day, he wondered how to explain it to her. Finally he decided to cross that bridge when and if he came to it. He had often heard his father say that women were born to complicate the lives of men, and now he realized his father was a very wise man.

Bess was waiting for him after the last class. "Where should we start looking?" she asked. "I was wondering about that swamp this side of the lake."

"We'll cover twice as much ground and waste less time if we hunt for him separately," he assured her. "Why don't you keep looking on your side of town, and I'll look on mine."

The plan made sense to her and they parted. Henry cut across the athletic field. He knew where he was going first: To a place where there were plenty of cats. If his Beagle liked to chase cats, and what dog didn't?, he would find plenty to his liking at the home of Henry's secret friend, the Cat Woman.

So far as Henry knew, he was her only friend. She lived alone on a hill about a mile from his home, and once or twice a week he made it a point to visit her. The Cat Woman's home was a three-room log cabin, well-built but lacking all modern utilities. There were no close neighbors and she only ventured outside the cabin on special occasions: To collect provisions left at the gate; to feed her army of cats; or to visit with Henry, when he appeared in the yard. Miss

71

Cornelia Stuyvesant was her name, but hardly anyone called her that.

Although the Cat Woman had been a resident of Green Valley for over twenty years, the people of that region knew very little about her. She was old, but no one knew how old. Some thought that it wasn't safe for her to live in the hills without such blessings as lights, gas and television. She paid her few bills promptly and by check—and no checks ever bounced, even though they were drawn on a San Francisco bank. Other people criticized her for playing hostess to so many cats, but the cat lovers defended her. Henry found her to be a very interesting person and he enjoyed playing with her cats. The cats enjoyed his attention, too. Otherwise, the Cat Woman would not have tolerated Henry's being there.

On this day he said, "I notice you have some planks in the shed."

"Yes, I have planks there," agreed the Cat Woman. "Also boards and nails and tools. I don't use any of the things in there. Do you want the shed?"

"Oh, I don't want anything, but I would like to borrow some planks. I'll return them. I want to build something."

"A boat?"

"No. A trap."

"And what do you wish to trap?"

"A dog. A little dog. Planks would be better than boards. Planks are heavier, you see. He wouldn't be able to move a heavy trap."

"Very well, so long as you plan to trap a dog. That would be moral and quite proper. But don't trap a cat."

"I wasn't thinking of that." Henry assured her.

"Never trap a cat. That would be a flagrant abuse of God's

72

will. People who trap cats are responsible for the coming of the end."

She had been predicting "the end" ever since Henry had first known her, and he still didn't know what end she was talking about, and felt that it would be impolite to ask. Besides, she talked to him as if he were a grown man, and he didn't want to lower his status. So now, instead of asking about the end, he changed the subject and asked, "Do you ever have trouble with dogs?"

"Never. I have nothing to do with them."

"I mean, do dogs ever chase your cats?"

The Cat Woman smiled and said, "Peace is like the night. One cannot touch it, yet it is there."

"It certainly is," he agreed. She was talking over his head again, and there wasn't much hope that he'd get a straight answer, but he took a chance and asked, "If you ever see a little black and tan and white dog anywhere around here, will you tell me?"

She walked to the cabin, opened the door and said—without so much as a glance toward Henry, "I'll tell you, but I will not talk to him!" Then she entered the cabin and closed the door behind her.

Henry remained in the yard, separating the good planks from the rotted ones. He planned to build the box-trap right there in the Cat Woman's yard, and later he would haul it to a likely place—by sled if there was snow, and trap the Beagle.

He had the plans for the trap pretty well organized: It would be oversized, so that when it fell over the unsuspecting dog no part of it would touch him; it would not hurt the Beagle nor would he be able to escape from it. The frozen ground would prevent digging; but, just to be sure, the boy planned to cover the ground area with heavy, flat stones. He was even thinking of fitting the inside of the trap with foam rubber, but didn't know where he could get it.

The boy worked until dusk, removing rusted nails and marking the best planks for lengths. He was home well before dinner, and Josie was pleased to find him so cooperative; first he carried water to the gaggle of geese, the big, gray birds who earned their keep as official garden weeders and unofficial guardians of the Deane acres; then he washed and combed his hair without so much as a reminder, helped set the table and even dried the dishes later. She was happy with her son's new image, and he was happy because he had a couple of good things going for him: Mental telepathy and a trap in-the-building. How could he miss?

It had been a satisfactory day for Murphy, too. Hunger pains had awakened him before dawn, and the quest for a meal became the first business of the new day. The sun was just coming up when he spotted a foolish hen roosting on the bottom rail of a fence. She came from some farmer's flock. The Beagle grabbed her by the neck as she slept and dragged her into the woods. Her feathers got in the way, but she made a fine meal. The pup even sampled a few of her bones and found them savory.

The hound wandered through the day, again without any sense of direction. Fortune guided him back toward Green Valley, even though the course was devious. At one time he was within a half mile of the old Thompson farm and the hideout he was seeking. Murphy stopped to rest in a hemlock grove. The landscape seemed vaguely familiar, and he was almost sure he had been there before. Then he was very sure, for he heard water rippling over the stones in a shallow stream. He went to the stream, lapped the water, then sat down to study the surroundings.

He barked for the first time in two days. It was a bark of victory. At last he had found the hideaway! He was so close.

Murphy waded through the stream and ran—his wagging stern failed to slow him. But he ran in the wrong direction. Minutes later he was lost again.

For the first time in his life, the confused Beagle pup felt overwhelming sadness. He sat down in the middle of an open field and howled. Would he ever see King again? He had tried so hard to find his leader and now—after all his efforts—he was in the middle of nowhere.

He didn't see the speck in the sky—a bald eagle—but the speck saw him. The eagle was migrating south and in no great hurry, and he had paused to circle about and investigate the chances of a meal below. The movement of some sort of life in the field had come under his surveillance, and now he went into swift descent for a closer look.

Murphy never saw him coming; he didn't even sense the danger. All perils were on the ground as far as he was concerned, for King—too huge to tempt an eagle—had taught him nothing about the sky.

A hundred feet above the ground the eagle spread his wings for brakes and screamed his bitter disappointment. The last thing he wanted to dine on was one of those things like Murphy—he had tangled with one when he was younger, and had been lucky to fly off still free but hungry.

In the same split second, the sorrowful Murphy saw the shadow of the spread wings and heard the terrifying scream. He jumped and ran for the woods. The pup did not know what he was running from and he didn't care. His sorrow had instantly turned to fright, and he was still trembling when he dove under the shelf of a protruding rock, to crouch and listen for the pursuit that did not come.

He was very cautious for the rest of the day and left the protection of the woods only to cross the roads. Twice he saw plump hens that would have made easy conquests, but Murphy wasn't hungry. He felt half sad, because he didn't know where to go or how to find King, and he was half-happy, because he was still alive.

Along toward midnight, weariness dictated his need for more sleep. A small building loomed against the sky directly before him. He crawled under it, curled up and went to sleep. He had not noticed any human scent, but there were other scents that seemed familiar and harmless.

The building was a small storage shed that was hidden on three sides by trees. Murphy had approached the shed from the rear. The shed faced an open yard, and a hundred feet across the yard was a three-room cabin where the Cat Woman lived.

✄ ✄ SEVEN ✄ ✄

MURPHY OVERSLEPT. HE WAS awakened in mid-morning by the complaining mews of several cats. They were well fed cats, but it was now another day and they were hungry.

The Beagle crawled out from under the shed and watched the scene unfold across the yard. An elderly woman appeared from the cabin. She was carrying a round, metal washtub. The cats quieted down and watched as she placed the washtub on the ground. She made several trips back into the cabin, pausing after each reappearance to pour or spoon things from pans into the tub. Then, she spent a few minutes stirring the contents of the tub. Finally she clapped her hands and shouted, "Come and get it!"

Her forty-odd cats made a dash for the tub. Some were big enough to put their heads over the side, others jumped in. They did very little talking. The Cat Woman watched to make sure that none of her charges were missing, then disappeared into the cabin and closed the door behind her.

Murphy found the drama engrossing. He had never had any trouble with cats, and the two he remembered best of all were among his earliest friends. But he did not know quite how to go about a mass introduction, so he sat and watched with admirable restraint.

A short while later most of the cats wandered away from the tub, and the entranced Murphy wondered what on earth he had been waiting for. He was hungry, too. He trotted to the tub, stuck his head over the side and started licking the remainders of the feast. Two small cats were still in the tub, but they paid no attention to him. A big, gray female walked over to him and rubbed her body against his, purring. Not a single cat was disturbed by his presence. It may have been a miracle, or it is possible the cats knew all about the safety in numbers theory.

Unknown to Murphy, his arrival had been seen by the Cat Woman. When she opened the cabin door again, he trotted off a short distance, watching her all the way. But she did not come to chase him. She carried a small bowl of food and placed it on the ground. When she spoke Murphy sensed that her words were meant for him: "I recognize you, kind sir. You are not really a dog. You are a messenger. So the end of the world will be soon? I knew it, and I am ready. We are all ready. Thank you, weary messenger."

She went back into the cabin and closed the door. Murphy and the big, gray cat investigated the bowl together. It was full of canned cat food. The two of them ate it, and Murphy gulped down the most.

He was giving the bowl a final, grateful lick when the woman opened the door and asked, "How do you spell your name? I want to tell somebody about you."

The Beagle knew she was talking to him. He sat down and cocked his head and looked up at her, and then he yawned. It seemed to satisfy the woman. She withdrew and closed the door.

He yawned again. The big, gray cat rubbed against him and purred. He lay down and closed his eyes, but his belly was too full for comfort, so he rolled on his side. The cat curled up between his legs. He didn't open his eyes, but he could feel her there and hear her gentle purrs. Soon they were both asleep.

Murphy was enjoying the luck of the Irish. He had stumbled upon a heavenly sanctuary, complete with shelter, food and four-footed companions.

How many cats did the Cat Woman own? Nobody really knew, and the only qualified authority on the subject was Thad Taylor, proprietor of Taylor's Village Superette. Every Friday, Thad delivered her weekly order in person. In addition to provisions for herself, the Cat Woman's order always included one case of evaporated milk and two cases of canned cat food, or enough to feed forty to fifty cats.

Thad always placed the order on the ground outside the Cat Woman's front gate. Then he covered everything with a canvas tarpaulin left there for that purpose. Next, he reached into the mailbox that never contained mail and withdrew a sealed, unmarked envelope. It always contained Miss Stuyvesant's check for last week's bill, and her order for next week's delivery. He never admitted to anyone that he had not seen Miss Stuyvesant in nine years, and had never even been in her yard. He did know that every Friday before

79

nightfall she would make several trips with a wheelbarrow and remove the food from the front gate.

He did not see Murphy on the first Friday of the dog's stay at the Cat Woman's place. It was raining that day, and Thad didn't even see many cats around. The only thing different about the yard was a big, half-built box or crate or something over by the shed. He wondered about that, but it was none of his business. When he got back to the store and opened the envelope, he forgot all about the box-like thing. Something new had been added to the order for the next week: Two cases of canned dog food. He had never seen a dog on her place, and he experienced a strange feeling: Wouldn't it be just like the old lady to be putting out food for stray dogs; and what if those dogs were the wild pack dogs that had jumped the Poodle people? Nobody could have told the old woman about those dogs!

After much thought, Thad had convinced himself that he was in danger of losing one of his most valued customers. When the sheriff dropped in to pick up some flour, Thad told him about his hunch.

"Wouldn't worry, if I were you," said Peter Long. "No sign of the pack dogs for almost a week now. Probably still running from those shots fired at the Wilson place. Say, come to think of it, I'll be up her way today. I'll talk to her."

"Thanks, Peter. Oh, if she won't talk to you, just leave a note for her in the mailbox. She'll find it."

The sheriff meant to call on the Cat Woman, but first he went home for lunch first, and there something happened to change his plans for the rest of the day. Sam Hawthorne was waiting for him.

"I think I've located the hideout of the pack dogs. Up at the old Thompson farm!"

"Great! Now why didn't I think of that spot myself, Sam? When did you find it?"

"Oh, a few days ago, I guess."

"Days? Why did you wait until now to tell me?"

"Hard to explain, Peter. Wanted to be sure, I suppose. Want to take a look today?"

"Right now! Let's go!"

So the sheriff didn't warn the Cat Woman about the pack dogs. Nor did anyone else.

After lunch that Saturday, Henry visited the Cat Woman's place. He patted a few cats and started to work on his trap. Then the Cat Woman joined him and they discussed his progress.

"A few more hours and I'll have it finished." said Henry. "This will be the safest trap ever made." She wanted to know how it would work, and he explained the operation.

"It's a wonder somebody hasn't thought of this before," she said.

"Oh, this is a very old idea. It's not mine."

"You are a very modest young man," she said. "If the end was not coming soon, I would convert you into a Believer."

He didn't hear her. His eyes were popping. "Why, what's wrong, Henry?" A Beagle was trotting across the yard. The tail-wagging dog trotted right up to the boy. There was no doubt in Henry's mind. This was the Beagle that had inspired the trap. He got down on one knee and patted the dog. Murphy licked his hand.

"I would introduce you," said the Cat Woman, "but it's quite obvious that you have met before."

"Is this your dog?"

81

"No, he is God's."

"Oh! But where does he live?"

"Here. He arrived just the other day. But he's really not a dog. He's a messenger."

"He doesn't have a collar," said Henry. "I wonder what his name is."

"Messengers don't have collars," she explained. "I've asked him his name several times, but he hasn't told me yet. He will, I'm sure. He's just waiting for the right time. You do understand, Henry?"

The boy nodded, but his mind was in total confusion. This was his Beagle! He knew it, he knew it! He had to own this dog. She had found him first, but she had once indicated that she didn't like dogs, so perhaps she would give the Beagle to him. It was certainly worth the try—no telling what the Cat Woman would say or do. "I would like to own this dog," he said. "I want him very, very much. I will give him a wonderful home."

"I believe you, Henry, and you must believe me. You are young, and you don't see things the way I see them. So believe me, this is not a dog. This is a messenger and I've been waiting for him for a long time. A messenger has no need for a wonderful home. Besides, you have already arranged to own a dog."

"I have?"

"Yes. You told me this trap would catch you a dog."

"Please!" he implored. "Please, please try to understand. This dog—this dog right here—is the one I planned to trap. This is the one I want. Will you give him to me?"

"But this dog really isn't a dog, you see, and he also belongs to God. How can I give you something that I don't own? God owns him. I'm so sorry, because I see you love him, but that's the way it is and the way it must be to the very end."

Henry stayed all afternoon, playing with Murphy. The trap was forgotten. He never completed it.

The boy lay awake for a long time that night, scheming one approach after the other. How could he win the Beagle from her? She was so unpredictable. Sometimes, he felt, she didn't even know what she was saying. He would just have to bide his time. Tomorrow, or the next day, or some other day, she might suddenly say that he could have the Beagle. On the other hand, she might never change her mind. He could not dislike the Cat Woman, but he wished she wouldn't live too long so he could have the Beagle.

On the drive to the old Thompson farm, Sam told Peter Long just how he discovered the pack's hideout. He carefully avoided any mention of the Beagle, and he told his story well—for he had carefully gone over just what he would tell the sheriff. He saw no point, either, in mentioning the time he had shot at the pack dogs and there were no pack dogs. If he had, and Peter repeated that story, Sam would never have lived it down.

Sam told about the family picnic—which was true—and about showing Bess the old barn foundation, which was also true, and about seeing old bones and not mentioning them because he didn't want to frighten the girl, which was not true. "Pack dogs didn't cross my mind at the time," he explained, "because then I hadn't heard about what went on at the Wilson place." That was true enough, and so were

83

the things he said about having a hunch and returning on another day and finding the tracks by the stream, and the path, and finally the hideout.

Peter didn't interrupt him even once, but he had never heard Sam talk so smoothly, and he felt that Sam had planned just what to say. Was he hiding something? And if he was, why?

"So that's it, Peter, that's all I know," concluded Sam.

"But you didn't see any of the dogs?"

"Nope. But the tracks aren't too old, and there are plenty of 'em. Three or four dogs, I'd say."

"Maybe this is a different pack, then. Mrs. Wilson said seven or eight."

"And maybe Mrs. Wilson can't count," chuckled Sam. "Wait 'til you see those big paw prints. Giant-sized. They have to be King's."

They parked the car a half mile from the farm and went their separate ways, guns at the ready. "Now be careful and don't shoot me," was Peter's parting warning.

Ten minutes later, according to plan, they crept from the woods and approached the old barn foundation. Sam came in from the south, Peter from the north. When they were out in the open they took turns advancing a few feet at a time. They were both alert, both tense, and they didn't make a sound. And both were disappointed when they got to the target area because the hideout was empty.

"Probably away on a little pleasure trip burning down homes and robbing banks," the sheriff commented. "But look at these strands of golden hair here. The yellow dog has been shedding. And my God, just look at all the bones! It's a wonder there's any livestock left in the county."

Then they visited the stream and Sam pointed out where he'd seen the biggest number of new prints.

"Four dogs at the most," Peter judged. "These big ones must be King's. And you know, Mrs. Wilson was right about there being a Beagle. Look here at these small, round prints."

They went downstream for a hundred yards, and there on the bank were fresher tracks made by a single dog. They had been made by Sport when he was looking for his friends and found the lamb chops. "I hate to admit it," said Peter, "but these could have been made by a Setter. A Setter-sized dog anyway."

As they walked back to their car Sam asked, "Think we should come back after dark?"

"No, we left our scent all over the place, so they won't come close for a few days now. But I think I know how to handle them. I'll let you know if I need any help."

The sheriff's plan was beautiful in its simplicity. From his examination of the old bones around the hideout, he knew that the favorite dishes of the pack dogs were lamb and fowl. Late the next day, armed and alone and wearing rubber boots and gloves, he returned to the old farm and scattered several lamb shanks and a few chicken quarters on the ground near the barn foundation. Every shank and every quarter was laced with deadly poison.

He disliked doing it, but it was a handy way of cutting down the pack's population. He represented the taxpayers and he felt he was doing his duty.

The small game season was legally open and in full swing. Landowners who objected to some fool hunters—who shoot

at anything that moves, and who think cows are wild game—
had the moral support of King and Rover. The two big dogs
hated the sounds made by all the shooting. The gunfire made
them nervous and increased their caution. The shooting
sounded personal. An open game season meant nothing to
them. Their legal season was year 'round.

They retired to the deep wooded hills on the perimeter of
Green Valley and temporarily adjusted their living habits
to a more normal pattern; action by day, sleep by night. It
was safer to keep their eyes open on the men with the guns.

From annual experience, they knew that all the shooting
would end some day. When that day came, there would be
sufficient snow on the ground to establish winter headquar-
ters at the lake. Until then, King and Rover were content
to keep on the move, trusting to luck that they would find
dry shelter for the night under rocks or fallen trees, or in
some long-unused farm building. They made a point of staying away from the old Thompson farm, and thus had no way
of knowing that the Setter continued to make midnight
visits there in the hopes of reestablishing contact with them.
Sport missed them. A house pet's life can be dull. He would
have been sadder still had he known that the big pack dogs
—and King in particular—did not miss him.

The black dog had never rated the Setter very highly.
Sport was a fun lover and a fine companion, yes, but he
could not be counted on. Sometimes he showed up and
sometimes he didn't.

But King missed the Beagle. He had not forgotten
Murphy's capture by the people at the stream, and felt sure
that someday he would find the little fellow. He genuinely
liked him. Then, too, the cold nights would be coming—the

hens would be roosting inside—and Murphy was small enough to get through those little doors. So the leader searched as he roamed. He saw a number of Beagles, but never Murphy.

Since King knew the countryside well, he was familiar with the Cat Woman's place. It was just about midway between the old farm hideout and that other place where the big hens with the very long necks lived. But the black dog was not interested in cats, for they had savagely damaged his self-esteem in his long ago puppyhood. He would starve rather than eat a cat, and he had never known the time when he was in any danger of starving. So he stayed clear of the Cat Woman.

Perhaps to compensate a bit for what he was sure was only the temporary absence of the Beagle, King let a black and white mongrel who was a little bigger than Murphy into the pack. The newcomer wore an old leather collar with nameplate attached. The collar was older than the dog and almost rotted through at several points. Etched on the nameplate was the bearer's name, Mutt. Below it was the name and address of the owner in New Jersey.

Somebody who knew breeds could have told at a glance that Mutt's family tree included many Terriers. He was a tough, smart, cocky fellow, a lover of fights and trouble. And as his master had sadly learned, the dog was also an incurable wanderer. When Mutt was much younger, he had frequently absented himself from home to explore the world. The dog sometimes returned of his own free will, and at other times was found by people who notified the master. Two years before he discovered Green Valley, Mutt returned home from a long trip to find that the master was absent. He had moved to another state, and they never saw each other again. Since that time, Mutt had been on his own, and lucky to be alive.

If he had been content to mind his own business, Mutt would not have met the big dogs. The refugee from New Jersey was chewing on a freshly killed rabbit when he noticed the two trotting through the woods. They did not see him. Mutt barked just to let them know that the rabbit was his. King and Rover investigated the source of the bark. It was late afternoon and they had just started to hunt for food. King had pheasant on his mind, but Rover was not particular. The yellow dog growled his intention to steal the rabbit, and Mutt lunged at the intruder. The woods were suddenly filled with the sound of fury. King waited for the right opening to lend Rover his support. A shot sounded, then another, and another. A hunter homeward bound had been attracted by the battle sounds. He had missed shots at squirrels and rabbits all day, and now he missed the dogs.

Mutt was no stranger to gunfire, and he could run—for a short distance anyway—almost as fast as the big dogs. By the time the three felt it was safe enough to pause, the rabbit was forgotten and there was no real reason to continue the fight. All three needed a drink and King led the way to a nearby stream.

He knew precisely where he was. The little stream ran its course along the base of a cliff. There was a path to the top of the cliff, and the black dog had been there many times on his scouting trips. From the top, there was an excellent view of a cornfield, gardens, and the roof of a house. It was in the cornfield that King had first spotted the big hens with the long necks. He wondered if they were still available.

The leader bounded across the stream and started up the

path. Rover and the new member Mutt swung in behind him. They stopped at the top, scanning the countryside. King walked away from the others and studied the cornfield. Yes, he could see several of the strange hens waddling between the neatly stacked sheaves. And there was a woman with them. She seemed to be talking to the fat hens.

Mutt saw her, too; he barked.

King snarled and drew back his lips. Mutt got the message and did not bark again.

In the cornfield, Josie Deane turned around and studied the brink of the cliff. Had she heard a dog bark? A single bark? Or was it her imagination? She couldn't be sure. Was that a dog up there, or was it a rock?

EIGHT

MURPHY CONSIDERED IT the almost-perfect life. Plenty of cat friends, a nice old woman, suitable amounts of tasty food, and now a boy to play with every afternoon.

It wasn't absolutely perfect because he still missed King. But, unlike King, who searched for him in aimless fashion, the Beagle looked for the black dog with concentrated purpose.

Around midday, he would search the woods and fields and neighboring hills with the hope of finding the black dog, or at least finding a familiar landmark that would point the way to the old farm. Murphy's journeys were never longer than one hour or so. The explorer could not forget his position at the Cat Woman's place.

He was away on just such an exploration when Thad Taylor arrived on the first Friday. If he had known that Thad was coming, he most certainly would have been on hand to supervise the delivery of the weekly order. For Murphy was feeling very responsible. He had broken up a few cat fights merely by barking, and all of the cats now regarded him with respect. The big gray one and a couple of others even slept with him under the shed, and more would have if he indicated any desire for their company.

He was aware, of course, that there was nobody else around to take care of the old woman. He would defend her to the death. Defense was all he really had to offer. He was anxious to please her; and he did, especially after the boy started visiting. The boy taught Murphy to retrieve an old tennis ball; and, when the old woman came out of the cabin and threw the ball for him, the dog brought it back to her as fast as he could run. Murphy sensed that she was very pleased.

One day was pretty much like another: A fine meal in the morning; a little loafing; a journey here and there; a complete check of the premises; a nap; playing ball with the boy; and then nothing much to do until nightfall and sleep.

Every so often at dusk, there was something special to do: The old woman would make several trips from house to gate and back again, pushing a wheelbarrow. Murphy would accompany her as she pushed, loaded, pushed and unloaded. Usually, there were three or four such trips.

One evening, Murphy figured that it was the right time again for the Cat Woman to push the wheelbarrow. Indeed, he was sure, for she always did it when the things were piled outside the gate. He checked and saw that the supplies were there. He went to the cabin door and waited. He barked, but the door did not open. The empty washtub and his own empty bowl were still outside, where the Cat Woman had filled them hours before.

The Beagle sensed that things were not as they should be. It had been a very strange day; even the boy didn't come to play with him.

There was nothing strange in that, really. Henry had told him the day before that he would be spending the weekend in Boston with his parents visiting friends, but the words meant nothing to Murphy.

When night descended, it was solid black—no moon, no stars. The cats had found their beds and were asleep, but Murphy continued to sit in front of the cabin door. He was a very puzzled dog.

At a late hour, he tilted his head back slowly, as far as the clean sweep of his neck would permit, and howled.

His sounds were not precisely those of a bugler playing taps, but they were close enough.

The door of the cabin stayed closed. The washtub and the bowl remained empty. The tarpaulin continued to cover the supplies by the front gate.

It was this way for three days. And the cats objected. Their mews turned into wails that filled the days and nights. Murphy had never heard such dreadful sounds and finally gave up his barking commands to cease wailing. The cats were hungry and refused to recognize authority.

Murphy knew they were hungry. He was hungry himself. On the third morning, he decided to do something about it. The cats were blaming one another for the lack of food, and fights were breaking out all over the yard. The Beagle trotted off to get away from the noise and to appease his stomach.

While he was still within sight of the yard, his nose picked up the fresh scent of rabbit. He found what he was seeking not far away and satisfied his appetite. Murphy was content; but, as he trotted back to the yard, a feeling of guilt assailed him. The cats had permitted him to share their handouts, yet he had done nothing in return. A way of expressing his thanks seemed in order. When another rabbit broke from cover directly in front of him, he bounded to the chase and returned victorious.

The little dog proudly carried the warm body to the center of the yard and dropped it on the ground. He intended to bark an invitation to eat but that was not necessary. The cats tore into his gift in a frantic, greedy manner and soon pieces of rabbit were all over the yard and there were more cat fights than ever before. Only the big, gray female, his special friend, remained peaceful. She sat by the empty washtub, delicately licking one paw. She had caught and consumed a songbird in his absence, but to Murphy she was the only cat present with manners.

His charity did not improve the general situation. The cats continued to complain, and it seemed to Murphy that most of the complaints were directed to him. Didn't they know that things had changed? Maybe they wouldn't get any more free handouts.

Murphy would protect them, but he didn't think he would ever feed them again.

Something was bound to happen. It always did. Maybe the boy would come today.

It was Thad Taylor who came.

One of his first customers on Monday had remarked that the Cat Woman's weekly order was still under the tarpaulin

94

outside the front gate. "Happened to drive by and noticed it there," he told Thad. "Hope there's nothing wrong."

As soon as he could break free, Thad drove to the Cat Woman's place and sure enough, there on the ground, was last Friday's delivery. He sat in the truck and blew the horn and shouted, but the only answering sounds came from the cats.

He got out of the truck and stood before the gate. The right thing to do would be to go to the cabin and knock on the door, but he had never been invited inside the gate and had no desire to offend one of his best customers. But something was wrong, and somebody had to find out what. He thought it would be a good idea to let the sheriff handle it.

On the other hand, maybe nothing was wrong. Maybe the Cat Woman was just off schedule. He doubted that she even had a calendar, but perhaps she'd appreciate knowing that somebody was concerned about her. Most customers would.

Thad stooped and picked up a piece of broken limb. He didn't know much about cats, and the thought did cross his mind that maybe they were trained as watchcats, like watchdogs. Watchdogs? That reminded him of his earlier hunch about the pack dogs. He looked around for a sturdier weapon and found a two foot length of rusted, iron pipe. With the pipe in his hand, he opened the gate and started up the dirt path to the cabin.

The cats ceased crying and moved away at his approach. He felt a little braver. Then he heard a bark and turned to see a Beagle charging at him from across the yard. Thad had often heard that tail-wagging dogs don't bite, and that barking dogs don't bite, but this one was doing both.

"Holy Mother!" he said aloud, "the killer Beagle!" He

threw the pipe at the oncoming dog, crossed himself, and ran full speed ahead for his truck. He made it with fifty feet to spare, turned on the motor and sped away.

Murphy halted outside the gate and watched the truck disappear down the road. Attack had not been on his mind. He had simply wanted the man to know that he was the Cat Woman's guardian. Still, it was a real feat to instill fear in something that big!

The dog turned and trotted up the path and across the yard to the shed. The cats regarded him with new respect. His trot resembled a strut.

And all the while, Thad Taylor was imagining all sorts of wild things. If only he had brought a gun! What a chance to be a hero! Meantime, where the dickens would the sheriff be?

Within the hour, Thad was speeding back to the Cat Woman's place as a passenger in Peter Long's car. He closed his eyes as the car skidded around curves, for the sheriff was driving and paying no attention to the miles-per-hour signs.

"This is one of tho e trouble days the world can do without," said Peter. "Knew it the moment I found Sport dead in the woodshed this morning."

"I can't figure who could have poisoned him, Peter."

"I don't want to know. I might kill him! Somebody must have tossed a piece of poisoned meat into my yard last night. Somebody holding a grudge against me, maybe. Some people think that laws are made for everybody else, and when they break them, I'm supposed to look the other way." He was thinking of the irony of it all: Some fool had poisoned

96

his Setter, and he himself was trying to poison the pack dogs. The irony ran deeper than that, but he would never know—never even suspect—that poor old Sport, the Setter with a private life, had again visited the old Thompson farm during the night and had eaten the poisoned banquet spread there by Peter's own hand. "Maybe I deserved this," said Peter.

"Deserved what?"

Peter didn't explain. Now he saw the dirt road that wound up the hill to the Cat Woman's place. He braked, turned the wheel sharply, stepped on the gas and set his mind to the business at hand. "You just saw the Beagle, Thad? No other dogs?"

"I didn't wait to look for any others! I got out of there real fast!"

"You can bet the others are around there, somewhere. Okay, you take the .45 and I'll use the shotgun."

"I've never handled a pistol," confessed Thad.

"Then I'll use the pistol."

"Can you hit anything with it?" When the sheriff did not reply, Thad continued, "I'm sorry. Say, if you don't mind, Peter, I'll follow you."

The car skidded to a stop in front of the Cat Woman's place. The armed men jumped out and approached the gate. The sheriff whispered, "Chances are they have her trapped in the cabin. Remember, now, these dogs are vicious. Shoot at any damn dog you see. Okay, let's go."

The rescue party proceeded up the dirt path to the cabin. They walked very slowly and looked in all directions. Thad stayed about thirty feet behind the sheriff, and the shotgun he carried was pointed directly at the sheriff's back. They saw plenty of cats, but nothing else. The cats seemed to glide out of their way.

97

The sheriff stopped. "Come in closer," he said. "What are you holding back for?"

"Pay no attention to me," Thad told him. "I know what I'm doing. I'm protecting our rear. Go ahead."

They moved toward the cabin again and the sheriff said, "No sign of even one dog. Maybe you scared the Beagle off!"

"It was just the opposite. Never thought I could run that fast. I tell you. . . . HEY! LOOK OUT!" shouted Thad. He had spotted Murphy.

This time, the Beagle charged in silent fashion, with his tail wagging. He came from behind the shed and he was almost halfway across the yard before the men saw him. The sheriff dropped to one knee, sighted his pistol and shot twice. His grip was loose and the .45 almost jumped from his hand. Before he could sight and fire again, Murphy—never breaking stride—swerved and ran out of sight behind the cabin. Only the shed was wounded.

"Missed him, dammit! He knows what a gun is, that's for sure! THAD! COME BACK HERE! WHERE THE HELL ARE YOU GOING?"

Thad didn't hear him. He had tossed the shotgun aside and was sprinting for the safety of the car.

The sheriff ran around the cabin, hoping for at least one more clean shot at the Beagle. He didn't see the dog, but he heard him crashing through the brush that fringed the woods. He ran into the woods but he never caught sight of the dog, and after a hundred feet he knew that further pursuit was hopeless.

He stopped, stood still, and listened. No, couldn't hear a thing up ahead. That Beagle could run! He sat down on a stump and tried to catch his breath.

Then he heard something to his right. It sounded like an animal moving over dried leaves. He turned his head very slowly and waited. The sound came again. Something was in the brush at the foot of the big rock! As he watched, the something moved and he saw a patch of black behind a dense barrier of twigs. The black patch moved again and the sound came again.

Well, I'll be damned, thought the sheriff. The black dog King! Thought he'd ambush me, eh? He's brainier than Sitting Bull.

Peter brought his pistol up very carefully, never taking his eyes off the black patch for fear he'd lose it, and holding his breath all the while. He sighted carefully and fired rapidly —one, two, three. Then he jumped to his feet and waited. But he saw nothing, heard nothing. Suddenly, twigs snapped to his rear. He whirled and almost shot the oncoming Thad Taylor.

"I heard the shots," said Thad. "Did you get the Beagle?"

"No, he got away, but I think I got a friend of his. Come along, we'll take a look. Over by that big rock."

"If you don't mind, I'll stay right here," said Thad. "Yell if you need any help."

Peter nodded and reloaded his pistol. Then he walked to the rock and searched through the brush—and all that he found was a freshly killed black cat.

"Anything?" called Thad.

The sheriff shook his head and said, "Let's get back to the cabin and have a look around."

They returned to the cabin and found the door unlocked. Peter pushed the door open, and there was the Cat Woman on the floor.

She was fully dressed and dead.

"Poor woman," said Thad. "Those damn dogs scared her to death! Poor old woman."

Peter nodded. He was reading what she had written in crayon on the wall—THE END OF THE WORLD IS NEAR.

Henry was one of the last persons in Green Valley to hear about it. The Deanes had spent an extra night in Boston and had not returned until late Monday afternoon. So Henry did not attend school that day, and his mother did not go shopping. But George had driven to his office to check on the mail, and then to the service station for gas. It was there that Art Purdy told him about the Cat Woman.

The boy heard the bad news that night at dinner. Even then he almost missed it, for he wasn't listening very carefully. Josie and George talked on and on about the trip to Boston, and since Henry had been on the trip, their words held little interest for him. So he amused himself with private thoughts until, for no reason at all, he decided to concentrate on what they were saying:

"Madge never seems to change," Josie said, "but Sidney gets stuffier and stuffier."

"Don't forget he's a Yale man," chuckled George.

Josie started to laugh, then choked and stopped. "I'm sorry," she said, for her thoughts had changed. "Laughing at a time like this. The poor woman."

Henry didn't understand. He turned to his father and asked, "What poor woman?"

"The Cat Woman."

"I never met her, never even saw her," said Josie. "But I

think she was a kind person. It must have been horrible at the end—so alone and so frightened."

The boy could only stare from one parent to the other. He thought he knew what they were saying, but he didn't dare ask the question. For the first time in his life he didn't want to be right.

The lawyer sensed his son's anxiety and did his best to sound casual as he explained, "You were outside when I told your mother the news, Henry. The lady they called the Cat Woman was found dead in her cabin. She'd been dead two or three days. It was a heart attack, and the authorities think she was frightened by the same pack dogs that attacked Mrs. Wilson at Willdo Kennel. The sheriff found two of the dogs near the cabin and shot at them."

Henry closed his eyes, bowed his head and waited. He was afraid to ask if one of the dogs was a Beagle or if either of them had been hit. He waited, and then his father said:

"Apparently he missed both of them. One was the dog they call King, and the other was the Beagle. Art Purdy told me the whole story, and he got it from Thad Taylor who was there. And Purdy is furious. He thinks everybody is trying to ruin the reputation of the Beagle breed."

A long silence ensued. Josie was about to say something to Henry, but George shook his head, so she didn't. They just sat there, watching their son until he lifted his head and asked to be excused. He explained that he didn't want any dessert and thought he would get to his studies.

Josie waited until the door to Henry's room closed before remarking, "He looked so pale, so suddenly. Do you think he's coming down with something? It's not like him to refuse dessert."

"He was fine until he heard about the Cat Woman," observed George. "I don't know what it is, but there's some connection there."

"How could there be? Why should there be?"

"Well, he has something on his mind. I'll go up and talk to him later. Perhaps I can help."

"As his father, or as his lawyer?" asked Josie.

He tugged at one ear and asked, "Now just what did that mean?"

"There are times," she told him, "when you act as if you were Henry's lawyer, not his father. You forget that you are a father who happens to be a lawyer."

He thought about her words for a few moments, then replied, "You are super-critical of me tonight, my dear. The only reason I am not losing my temper is that you are probably right. I'll watch it."

Later, the father-lawyer climbed the stairs to Henry's room and knocked on the door.

"Come in," said Henry.

George entered and found the room dark. "Will it disturb your studying if I put on a light?"

"Please do."

The light revealed Henry sitting on a window bench, staring out into the night. The boy turned to his father and asked, "Anything wrong?"

"No, I just felt like talking," said George, sitting on his son's bed. "Can you think of anything to talk about?"

"Mom won't like it if she catches you sitting on the bed. I was thinking about all those cats, for one thing."

George switched to a chair and asked, "What about them?"

"They must be pretty hungry by now. Maybe we should go up there and feed them."

"I understand most of them have been rounded up and taken to an animal shelter. They'll stay there until the Cat Woman's will is read. I once heard that her will provided for them. I imagine she would do a thing like that."

"Yes, she was a very thoughtful person, and she loved her cats," said Henry.

"Did you know her?" asked George, realizing when he asked that he sounded like a lawyer. "I mean, did she know you?" It was a father's version of the same question.

"Yes," Henry confessed. "I'd see her sometimes on my way home from school. I thought of her as my secret friend. I suppose that's why I never told you or Mom or even Art Purdy about her. For some reason, a secret friend was important. Will you remember to tell me about her will? She would want her cats to be happy."

"I'll watch for the hearing. Had you seen her recently?"

"Last week. And I would have gone there on Friday, but we went to Boston."

"How did she seem to you?"

"Fine. The same as always. She said things that I didn't understand, but that was not unusual. She would say beautiful things that made no sense at all. Not to me, anyway. Dad, did you say the pack dogs killed her?"

"No. They say the pack dogs frightened her, and that's what brought on the heart attack that killed her. Did she ever mention seeing strange dogs around her place?"

Henry closed his eyes, as if trying to remember. Should he mention the Beagle? He decided against it and shook his head.

"Something is troubling you," George said. He paused before adding, "Will you let me help? What's wrong?"

"Nothing."

"I'll accept that in reference to the Cat Woman, Henry." The lawyer paused again, trying to find the right words, then he added, "My question was a general one, and really a change of subject. You know, I've been thinking a great deal about our new life in the country. A sort of summing up of our year away from the city. I think your mother is happier here. At least, I haven't heard her complain about missing anything. I don't quite know about myself. I'm healthier, that's for sure. I've been busy, and things are looking better. Too busy, perhaps, for you and I haven't had a real talk in a long time. Are you sorry that we moved, Henry? Do you miss your old friends?"

"Jerry Walker was my best friend. We write."

"Have you found any close friends here?"

"Friendships don't happen overnight," Henry told him. "The boys have different interests here, but I'm learning. They talk about horses, and fishing and hunting, and dogs. Things like that. Not city things."

"Well, I know next to nothing about horses, but you and I could fish and hunt together, for a start. Would you like that?"

Henry looked at his father for a moment before smiling and replying, "Yes, I think so. Thank you."

Then the phone rang downstairs, and they could hear Josie calling for George. Before leaving the room, he asked, "By the way, Henry, do you still want a dog?"

It was the silliest question Henry had ever heard, but he managed a polite yes. The boy not only wanted a dog, he wanted a particular dog—a certain Beagle. But how does a boy tell his father that the dog he wants is a pack dog, a criminal, a suspected accomplice in murder? Especially when his father is a lawyer.

Things had added up in Henry's mind, and he could no longer deny what he wished he could forget: His Beagle was the same pack Beagle. He had seen his dog's tracks mingled with others, he had seen him with other dogs, especially with the big black one, and he had even touched the wound on the little hound's right thigh.

It didn't lessen his love for the Beagle. He still wanted him. He would find him and somehow restore the dog to a rightful place in society: The Deane home.

He went to bed early, but he couldn't sleep. Whenever he closed his eyes, he saw either the head of his Beagle or the face of the Cat Woman. The message in the dog's eyes was easy to read: Come find me, come find me. But the woman's expression puzzled him, and he felt awful when he finally interpreted it: You wished that I would die, so that you could claim the little dog.

Henry wished that he could tell her the whole truth—that he hadn't really wanted her to die, that he had just wanted her Beagle. Now he wondered if he would always carry the guilt of her death in his heart.

So he kept his eyes open, which wasn't difficult, for now he was wide-awake. He could just see the dim shape of the apple tree, and to him it seemed darker in the room than it was outside. He left his bed and went to the window. There was no moon, but he could see as far as the garage, some seventy-five feet away. His Beagle, alone or with the pack, would have no trouble seeing his way around on such a night.

But where was his Beagle? Henry didn't know, but the thought struck him that the dog might still be in the vicinity of the cabin. And why not? Hadn't the little hound known happy days there, and wouldn't he think there might be

105

more in the future, especially if he didn't know his benefactor was dead?

In no time at all, Henry convinced himself that the Beagle was hiding somewhere near the cabin, staying out of sight so that no one would shoot him, waiting for the Cat Woman to return, even waiting for Henry Deane.

Henry dressed quickly in the dark and put a flashlight in his pocket. He tied his shoelaces together and hung the shoes around his neck. It was late and he was pretty sure his parents were asleep.

He crawled out the window and onto the roof of the porch. Then he crossed to a limb of the apple tree and worked his way to the trunk, where he dropped to the ground. He walked to the road in his stocking feet and then sat down to put on his shoes. Henry walked up the road toward the Cat Woman's place.

His mother's geese were the only witnesses to his departure, and only they saw him return, hours later, alone.

❧❧ NINE ❧❧

THE FARMERS ALMANAC predicted a very mild winter. But Green Valley's residents looked out their windows Thanksgiving morning, and saw snow five inches deep. They would not see the bare ground again until April.

It was the first snow experience for Murphy. He found it tasteless and lacking in substance. When he walked through it, it made his belly cold. It wouldn't go away so he had to accept it because it was there. It took him a few days to recognize the virtue of the stuff: It simplified hunting. Tracks were easy to see; and, if none were around, he didn't waste time utilizing his nose, wind or no wind.

Finding food was his only real problem, so he accustomed himself to eating at opportune times rather than on schedule. Small game was not as abundant as in previous months—hibernation and migration were not his concern—plump hens did nicely when nothing else was available. He considered roosters the same as hens. One could usually be found during the night, perched on a low limb or rail or on a log. It took cleverness and daring to succeed, for the prize was usually perched near a house. The whole trick was to carry off the still-squawking meal before the house lights were turned on. Murphy developed it into an art.

The lonely life did not appeal to him, but he was sure that he would run into King or the boy sooner or later. He had no idea how long it had been since the good days at the Cat Woman's place; but, just as his built-in compass kept him close to Green Valley, another sense told him that solitude was the wisest course for the time being.

The dog was wiser than even he realized. The fantastic tales woven by the Poodle breeder, the sheriff, and Thad Taylor were believed in entirety by many people, and the Beagle—almost any Beagle, for that matter—had earned an ugly reputation. Art Purdy saw to it that his dogs stayed penned in their runs, and they only ran free when he was with them. Some fool might shoot first and inquire about the Beagle's ownership later, and Art knew a lot of fools with guns.

Unaware of his own bad reputation, Murphy dashed across a field one late afternoon to celebrate a surprise reunion with a boy he had mistaken for Henry. He barked to announce his joyous coming, and the boy had ample time to gather stones and hurl them at him. All of the stones were thrown in fright, and all but one—a jagged one—missed the target. Murphy stopped and yelped in complaint when the stone bounced off his quarters. Was Henry out of his mind? The boy shouted and threw more stones. A second, closer look told Murphy that the boy was not Henry. The dog turned and ran away.

The youngster's unfriendly attitude puzzled the little hound, but it didn't deter him on another day when he thought he saw Henry walking with a little girl along a wooded path. Their laughter aroused him from his afternoon nap, and he broke from cover as soon as he saw the boy. There was gladness in his every bark, but the girl screamed and ran away and the boy stayed less than a step behind her. Murphy increased both his speed and the volume of his barks. The brave boy clambered up a huge rock and Murphy halted at its base. He was unable to climb the rock himself, so he sat on the ground and looked up at the boy. Then he realized that the boy was not Henry. It didn't matter. He would wait until the boy climbed down and played with him.

The boy and the dog maintained the status quo for more than an hour. Then Murphy heard the angry voices of approaching people. He retreated into the woods and the rescue party never saw him. But the party rescued the boy— and for weeks the young dramatist repeated the tale of how he had risked his life for the girl by distracting the vicious Beagle until the heroine had made her escape.

After those incidents, Murphy felt that it would be best to play it safe. Obviously, every boy was not Henry. Indeed, none of the others acted like Henry. The safest course was to trust his nose and not his eyes, and someday he would find the real Henry—or the real one would find him. There was plenty of time. He could wait.

And because of those incidents—and others that were the end results of pure imagination—the pack remained a current subject in Green Valley. The innocent Beagle became the pack's flag bearer, for people assumed that the little hound's associates were somewhere nearby. Murphy's reputation was beginning to rival that of King's, and the pup who was now old and wise for his months was beginning to irritate Peter Long—for there were people who joked about "the big sheriff who could not find the little dog."

Meanwhile the big black dog was shying from trouble and minding his manners, hoping that people would forget the pack. Murphy, in order to survive, was at times, a vegetarian. Deer trails led him to the spot where the graceful animals dined on the red berried clusters of scarlet sumac. All Murphy had to do was bark, and if the frightened deer broke some of the brittle sumac, the berries were within his reach for feasting. The scent of fox led him to the discovery of May apples and wild grapes. Once he watched in amazement as an old raccoon dug for the tubers of wild day-lilies washing each tuber, one by one. Murphy watched the strange performance until the raccoon started to eat the little tubers. Then the hound broke cover, chased the raccoon off, and claimed the remaining tubers. He found them chewy and tasteless, and never bothered a raccoon again.

Finally his wandering brought him to the lake where he had spent the summer. The sight of it meant nothing to him. He saw no familiar landmarks. The area he explored was at the far end, more than two miles from the city couple's cottage and on the opposite shore. It was all new to Murphy, although he wondered if he had ever seen similar buildings before.

He found the area peaceful and to his liking. Evidence of good hunting was everywhere and it seemed to be abandoned. The buildings provided a variety of shelters and he preferred the ones with stoops. The space under a stoop was confined and closed on three sides—ideal for a little dog who created his own warmth. And it was dry.

110

The Beagle was dozing under his favorite stoop on the morning Mutt discovered him. The cocky little mongrel was sniffing around outside, sure that there was a dog in the fort and wondering who the stranger was. The lake belonged to the pack and Mutt had appointed himself—for the moment —the pack's official representative. With the coming of the snow, King had led his followers back to the lake for the winter season.

Murphy heard the sniffing, but he didn't investigate until his nose told him that the sniffer was another dog. He scrambled out from under the stoop, pleased to discover that the black and white was not much larger than himself. He stepped up to the newcomer and sniffed him all over, delighted to make his acquaintance.

The mongrel stood at attention, stiff and alert, as the Beagle attended to the introductory ceremony. Suddenly, he lunged for Murphy's throat! The air was filled with their sounds of rage as the two engaged in combat. Mutt made most of the noise, but Murphy contributed his share.

The sounds of battle traveled across the lake and into the ears of the sleeping, big dogs. They awoke, and King saw that Mutt was missing. He cocked his head and listened to the distant noise. Then he looked at Rover. Both dogs were thinking alike: This was their land, and a strange dogfight was an insult to their status and possessions. Furthermore, anything that attracted the attention of outsiders to the lake was dangerous.

The big black dog and the yellow dog crawled out from under the cottage and ran across the frozen lake. They did not waste time looking for Mutt, but they found him anyway—engaged in a slashing, snarling brawl with a little black and tan and white dog. King bounded into the midst of the confusion—not to lend assistance to Mutt, but to break up the fight. They parted as soon as he landed between them, but Mutt continued to snarl his contempt for the Beagle. King picked up the mongrel in his huge jaws and deposited the scrappy black and white in the middle of a nearby bush. Then the leader turned to investigate the stranger who had the audacity to challenge the honor of the pack. He was pleasantly stunned when he recognized Murphy. The black dog lowered his head and Murphy licked his good ear. Then, for old-time's sake, King butted the Beagle to the ground and held him there under one of his huge paws. Murphy whined his delight.

From that day, the pack numbered four. Two big dogs and two little ones.

It was a most unusual pack, worthy of clinical study. The leader remained the leader. He placed his trust in Rover, but his affection—when he displayed it—was for Murphy. The Beagle was his favorite.

Rover didn't mind. He liked the Beagle, too, but he detested Mutt. He didn't trust the noisy, yappy, cocky, trouble-making dog who wore a collar. He wished that Mutt would disappear.

Mutt considered Rover a prince of a fellow. The mongrel knew that he didn't rate very high with King, and he didn't care. He devoted himself to the unappreciative yellow dog and never fully accepted Murphy. He felt that he could lick the Beagle, and he was jealous of the little one's hold on King. He was waiting for the right moment to knock the stuffing out of Murphy.

The Beagle adored King, he liked Rover and he tolerated Mutt. Murphy had no inkling that the mongrel was out to get him. While their battle had been short, he figured that

112

he had taught Mutt a fine lesson. Even if he had known Mutt's hatred for him, Murphy would not have worried. He had knocked around and taken care of himself, and figured that he was almost as big as Mutt, anyway.

Self-confidence was their common bond.

Art Purdy drew a bead on the doe and held his breath. He would have preferred a buck, but he had enough trophies on the wall; this doe was a big one, and venison was on his mind. She was standing in the open, on the side of a hill, about six hundred yards away. She seemed to be looking right at him, as if she knew something was wrong. Art squeezed the trigger. The doe took a few steps and slumped to the ground almost before the shot echoed through the valley.

She was the most obliging deer Art had ever shot. Why he could drive his car along the gravel road to within fifty feet of where she fell. He lit his pipe before starting for his car, then looked once more to be certain about the spot. All he saw was the doe's white flag as she bounded into the woods.

Art hurried down the grade, across the field, and up the hill to the spot where the doe had fallen. There was blood on the snow, and more blood spattered along her tracks. He hated to admit it, but he had to: The slug had missed her heart and her lungs, and probably ripped through her abdomen. No telling how far she would run, or how long she would live. He shrugged and followed her tracks. It was hard going through the snow, but Art Purdy wasn't one of those poor sportsmen the Conservation Department always complained about—those who wound a deer and let it run off to die. What a waste of life!

He followed the doe's tracks for almost two miles. By that time, he was winded and afraid that he might have a heart attack. The doctor had warned him about that. So he gave up his pursuit, returned to his car and drove home. He still felt the conservation people were right, but convinced himself that they were talking about younger hunters. Why, if he were twenty years younger, he'd still be following the doe. He decided not to tell the fellows about the incident. . . .

The doe was still running. She didn't understand the pain, but instinct had prompted her to run and fear kept her running. She was miles from the point where the slug had dropped her before she paused to rest. The doe was tired, and her very weariness puzzled her. It had not been that much of a run.

She went to her knees in the snow. The wet cold was comforting and seemed to ease the pain. She looked around, ever alert for danger. She saw her blood on the snow and didn't know it was her strength ebbing away. She would stay there until she sensed pursuit. She might even die there.

Pursuit was already in the making. The roaming pack had discovered her tracks and were studying them. Deer tracks were nothing new to the dogs, but these tracks were much more interesting—they were fresh with blood. Rover, Mutt and Murphy waited patiently for their leader's signal.

King was not in the mood for a long chase. The pack had been eating well and hunger was not pressing. He knew that most of the work would be up to Rover and himself, because Murphy and Mutt didn't have the legs for this sort of thing. It takes a number of dogs, alternating in the role of pressing the deer, to reach and bring the prize down. When the first dog tires and lags, the second dog takes over, and then the third, and then each in turn again. And the conditions this time weren't right, either. King preferred deeper snow. Deep enough to really hinder the prey.

Still, there was blood, and it was fresh. Part of the task was already accomplished. This deer was in no condition to run very far, and perhaps not for very long at top speed. This one might even be nearby.

King decided on a short chase. It was worth a try, for success meant a supply of meat for several days. He glanced at his followers, then trotted off on the trail of the doe. The other three swung in behind him.

The black leader moved along at a medium trot. He was in no great hurry, and would not be, until he caught sight of the deer. Then he would apply pressure.

After a few minutes, the foursome came to the doe's recent resting place. The wind had carried word of their coming, and she had renewed her flight without waiting for visual confirmation. Her body heat had melted the snow to the ground, and the dogs licked the blood that was still warm. The taste increased their enthusiasm.

King went to the trail again, but this time he set a faster pace with Rover. The two little dogs tried to stay with them but, within a few minutes, the big dogs were out of sight. The mongrel and the Beagle could only follow at a slower pace.

Ahead of them, the doe ran as fast as she could. Her course was not in a straight line, for she sought running room where the footing was best and avoided the drifts and the valleys. The doe knew that more than one dog was on her trail. Their barks, now and again, came to her on the wind. She was running for her life, and the strange feeling of

115

pain was almost unbearable. The barks sounded closer and closer, and she couldn't understand it, for she had outrun dogs many times in her three years.

The red on her tracks was her strength. She went on for over six miles; her speed slackened while her panic told her that she was moving ever faster. She raced upgrade through a dense grove of cedars, where the snow was light and a bed of old needles provided a welcome cushion. She listened, but heard no barks. Then she settled down with the feeling of being safe, but only for a few seconds. She sensed danger and looked around. A big black dog was rushing straight at her.

The doe struggled to her feet and ran. King ran at her side, growling, until she turned. He continued his pursuit at her heels, but made no attempt to bring her down. The black dog was herding the doe. He knew where he was and she didn't. The doe lost her footing and went over the edge of the cliff.

King stopped at the brink and watched the doe tumble over and over down the irregular face of the cliff. Twice she slammed into jagged rocks, and then she slid to the bottom. She lay on her side over the frozen stream. The big black dog found the path and took his time descending.

The doe's neck was broken and her body had quivered for the last time before the dog arrived. He slashed the throat first, so that he could drink the warm blood. Then he waited for his comrades. The chase had been longer than he anticipated, and he wanted to rest before the meal.

He didn't have to wait long for Rover. The yellow dog was ready for his meal, and King did not object as his loyal follower ripped into the doe's quarters.

Mutt and Murphy arrived a short while later. They had viewed the end of the chase from the brink, then moved down the path, with Mutt barking excitedly every foot of the trip. There was no way for King to quiet him. The mongrel would never learn to keep his mouth shut.

King snarled when Mutt was close enough to hear him, but that didn't stop the mongrel from barking or from circling the doe's body. He started showing off by challenging the lifeless doe to battle. King had to almost swallow Mutt's head before the little dog would quiet. The leader was the only one who remembered that there was a house not very far away.

Murphy sat down and watched the others. He was accustomed to eating last, and this time he wasn't sure he wanted to eat at all. He was tired and more thirsty than hungry. The snow had been much too deep for his short legs. After a few minutes, he started to investigate the frozen stream. He looked for an opening in the ice; and this led him to the edge of the cornfield, where he found himself not ten feet away from one of the strange, long-necked, big hens.

The gander had been attracted by Mutt's excited barks. He was investigating the source. This was his domain and trespassers were not permitted. The protective instinct of the Toulouse goose is just as strong as it was in the time of ancient Rome. The breed's legendary aggressiveness also remains intact. This gander would not spoil the legend.

He lowered his neck and stretched it out until his eyes were on a level with Murphy's. Then he whistled.

The Beagle was amused. He had never seen a hen so large or strange as this one, but he had the experience to handle the type. The thing to do was to grab the big hen by the neck and run. This hen was inviting trouble, and Murphy felt compelled to oblige.

As the gander whistled again and waddled closer, the confident Beagle lunged to the attack. He had sadly underestimated the size of his intended victim's neck and found his mouth choked with feathers. He crouched and lunged again and received a whack on his muzzle. The gander was ready for him the second time, and his bill had done the damage.

Murphy backed off to reconsider, and that was a mistake. The gander squawked to heaven and came at him with huge, pounding, hurting wings. The Beagle was knocked down and had no chance to regain his footing. The wings were clubs and the yellow bill was a dagger. The dog could only whine and cry. He had no defense. The gander kept coming at him, showing no mercy.

It was all over in minutes. The body of the helpless dog was still, and blood seeped from many wounds. The air was full of noise: Loud honks and squawks from the arriving members of the gander's harem; and loud trumpeting from the gander as he blew his victory call, again and again.

The peculiar sounds had been heard by the pack dogs, of course, but only King looked into the matter. Rover and Mutt were too busy eating. Anyway, the leader was expected to take care of anything that sounded important.

The black dog trotted into the open cornfield and stopped. For one of the few times in his life, he was utterly bewildered. Before his very eyes, a big hen was beating the life out of a very still Murphy. Other big hens were rushing to the scene. Their clamor offended his eardrums.

As he started for the hens, he heard voices. He stopped

short and saw a woman running across the field. She was shouting and coming his way.

Then he heard the oddest whistle. He turned his head to see the biggest hen of them all waddle straight for him, neck low and extended.

King decided to attack.

❦ ❦ TEN ❦ ❦

JOSIE DEANE HAD BEEN sitting at her desk for over an hour, and all she had to show for it were two words on paper: Dear Polly.

Her sister Polly lived in Paris—when she wasn't living in London, Rome or Athens—and she had written Josie the month before asking how things were going with the Deanes in Green Valley, and how they found life among the country bumpkins. Polly's world consisted of cities and smart society, and her letter had been almost too witty and condescending.

Josie had put off answering the letter until today because she just couldn't decide what news to report. Consequently, she had not progressed beyond the salutation.

Should she confess that she had never really liked city life and that now she loved the country; that now she could indulge in gardening to her heart's content and even had geese to help her, that she hadn't visited the city—for shopping or theatre or anything else—in almost a year?

No, for Polly just wouldn't understand. And inasmuch as she had never cared for George, there was no need to explain that he had been offered a senior partnership in the city law firm; that he had suffered a heart attack and the doctor had prescribed a slower pace. It would bore Polly to hear that the hospital bills had come to over three thousand dollars, or that George was healthy again and enjoying his small town practice, or that he kept a fishing rod in his car for use on slow days.

Dwell on Henry, then, and about how well he is doing in school, how he has developed the appetite of a horse, and how fast he is growing.

No, because Polly wasn't interested in children, not even her own.

I'll tell her to go jump in a lake, Josie decided. I'll tell her to stop looking down her nose at happy, normal, well-adjusted people.

But Josie didn't write a single word more, for just then the uproar from the gaggle of geese reached her ears. She listened, knowing that if it continued it would be wise to investigate. When the hullabaloo continued, she called out, "Henry, I'm going outside! The geese are after something again! Be sure to stay inside the house!"

"I heard them!" he shouted from his room. "I think they're somewhere in the cornfield!" Josie had kept Henry home from school that day, hoping to curb a troublesome cold. The boy was already standing at an upstairs window, focusing his father's field glasses.

Josie threw a coat over her shoulders, grabbed a broom and hurried out the door. She heard the trumpeting. It meant one of two things: Either the trouble was all over, or it was just really beginning. She ran for the cornfield.

She had purchased the gaggle of Toulouse the year before, when the geese were mere goslings. She wanted them as weeders, and they had more than proven their worth. But no one had told her about the true Toulouse personality: A quick temper, unpredictable moods, a violent dislike for strangers, and a strong urge to protect home grounds against all trespassers—man or beast, and sometimes a falling leaf or a sparrow. Just the past Sunday, the gaggle had chased an innocent pheasant hunter. The man had wisely climbed the nearest tree, and he would have shot them if he had not dropped his shotgun as he fled. George had laughed when he heard about the incident, and he had suggested that Josie post signs reading BEWARE OF MAD GEESE. Now, as she ran to investigate the gaggle's current activity, she thought the sign was not such a bad idea after all.

She saw the geese at the far end of the cornfield. Still running, she waved the broom and shouted at them. The geese were making too much noise to hear her, and she couldn't see what interested them.

But Henry had seen, through the field glasses. He had noted the presence of the black dog—the same one he had seen at the old Thompson farm! He knew that it was the infamous King. Then he saw his mother running for the field, and her only weapon was a broom.

The boy dashed down the stairs, paused at the hall closet just long enough to pick up his father's double-barreled shotgun, and hurried outside. Now, as he raced after his mother, he shouted for her to stop.

Up in the cornfield and still out of his view, Josie had already stopped. She had come within a hundred feet of the

123

black dog before she saw him, and the very sight of the huge animal terrified her. It must be King! She found it impossible to take another step, and she didn't think she could muster the willpower to scream. All she could do was watch with cold fascination as the black dog slowly lowered his body to a crouch and waited for the confident gander to waddle just a little closer. The dog seemed almost contemptuous of her presence. He did not even acknowledge her with a glance.

Then Josie heard her son's approaching shouts. She wanted to call out a warning for him to stay back, but her fear would only permit the thought.

Henry would have disregarded the warning anyway. He ran right past his mother, shouting at the top of his lungs. Then he halted and brought the shotgun to his shoulder and aimed at the black dog.

His target was already on the move. King had waited only long enough to determine what the boy was carrying. The object looked familiar, and he knew its meaning too well to tarry. He barked just once as he fled the scene—a warning signal that proved totally unnecessary, for Rover and Mutt had retreated into the woods at the first sound of a human voice. They had been watching, and when they saw their black leader race past the fallen doe and out of their view, they broke from their hiding place and ran after him.

Once again, Murphy had been abandoned.

Josie and Henry spotted the Beagle when he made a valiant attempt to get to his feet. Then the dog flopped on his

124

side in the snow, and all around him the white blanket was spattered with red.

Henry raced to the dog and cradled the little hound's bloodied head in his hands. They recognized each other—although Murphy's recognition was mostly by scent, and his greeting was no more than a faint whimper. The dog was weak and in pain and bleeding from a score of gander-inflicted wounds.

The boy looked at his mother and said, "He's in very bad shape . . . he'll die if we don't take care of him . . . he'll die, I know it!" His words weren't too distinct, for he wept as he said them, but Josie understood. Then Henry fell to his knees and hugged the dog. He wanted to reveal that this was his dog—and had been his dog ever since the Cat Woman died; but he did not know how to confess it or even if it would be wise. He was a very confused boy.

His mother knelt beside him in the snow and placed a hand on the dog's quarters. She could feel the body quiver. "Run as fast as you can and phone the vet," she directed. "Tell him it's an emergency, that we don't have a car, and that he must come here!"

"What about the black dog? You go."

"He won't return. Now don't argue, do as I say! And take the gun and put it back where you found it. Your father would be furious. Run!" She watched until he was out of sight, then picked up Murphy and draped him over her arms. He didn't weigh much and she could easily achieve a standing position.

The geese were standing around in a semi-circle, watching. They appeared interested and sympathetic. The gander flapped his wings as if to emphasize complete innocence.

"I was crazy to name you Walter Mitty," Josie said to him. Then she started to walk back to the yard, carrying Murphy as gently as possible. The gander waddled right behind her, and the females followed in single file behind their lord. The parade reminded Josie of the sacrificial ceremonies in ancient times, except that she wasn't offering a life—she was trying to save one.

When she reached the yard, a breathless Henry popped out of the new garage. Yes, the vet was on the way—there were towels on the work bench and the Beagle should be placed on them—he would be right back with hot water, more towels, cotton, tape and iodine.

Josie placed Murphy on the bench and waited for her son to return. The dog's eyes were open but glazed, as if he were in a state of shock. She hoped that the garage was warm enough, and was thankful that George had insisted on insulation and heat when they had built it, even if the extra expense had put off acquiring a second car. Then she noticed that the towels were her very best ones; the ones she used for guests. But this was not a time to complain—for all she knew, her boy had saved her life. So she said nothing about the towels when Henry returned with his hands full of first-aid accessories.

Together, they washed the dog's wounds and stopped most of the bleeding. A hastily improvised tourniquet halted the flow from an ugly rip on one foreleg. Through it all, Murphy was still and uncomplaining.

"We just have to save him," the boy said.

"Oh, we will, we must! I wish the vet would get here."

"He promised to hurry."

There was nothing else they could do, except wait and ponder private thoughts. Henry debated telling his mother about his relationship with this very Beagle. But he did not. And Josie felt a certain guilt, as if she were entirely responsible for what had happened. After all, she owned the geese. Then she thought of the black dog and shuddered, and that led her to ask, "Did you put the shotgun away?"

"Yes."

"Henry, I think I should be angry with you for being disobedient. You didn't remain in the house, and you knew you were not supposed to touch your father's gun. What are you doing without a coat? You have a cold, young man. March to the house and get a coat, now. Oh, did you remove the shells from the gun?"

"I tried to, Mom, but do you know what I discovered? It was unloaded all the time."

Josie smiled and closed her eyes. Had all this been a bad dream? Her hand touched Murphy's head. It was not a dream. "You and I are two very lucky people," she said to the boy.

"I know. I'll bet this Beagle brought us the luck."

She knew from past experience that the reasoning of the young is often beyond the comprehension of the old. But she nodded in agreement anyway, and asked him again to please get his coat.

"We've done all we can for him, now it's up to his own gods," said the vet.

"Will you take him back with you?" asked Josie.

"The less we move him the better, but it's up to you. He's not your dog. I'd understand."

"He stays," she decided, "and we'll bring him to the house when George gets home."

127

"No need for that, it you don't let it get too cold in here."

"Dad keeps it at fifty degrees," contributed Henry. "This is his workshop.

"Fine. Now, fix up a box or a basket for him. Raise it off the floor and keep him out of drafts. You can use old newspapers or rags for bedding, stuff you can throw away. He hasn't much blood left, but there may be a little more bleeding."

"What about a transfusion, Dr. Schutz?" asked Henry.

"Later on, maybe. I'll drop in for a look in the morning. Any idea who his owner is?"

"He didn't have a collar," Josie said. "Of course, it might have been ripped off in the cornfield."

"Suppose you and I stroll up there and have a look around, Henry?"

Josie objected. She wanted Henry to stay inside as much as possible and volunteered to accompany the vet herself. As the two walked to the field, she commented, "You're not much of an optimist."

"I think of myself as a realistic optimist," he said. "I didn't want to say too much in front of the boy and raise any false hopes, but I can tell you that the dog would be dead right now, if I hadn't given him that stimulant. Frankly, Josie, this dog has less than a fifty-fifty chance, but that may be enough. Dogs seem to have more stamina than most animals. Sometimes, they amaze you with their recuperative powers."

"Then you think he'll pull through?"

"I didn't say that. He has a concussion, and there's no telling if it's mild or severe. I don't think any ribs are broken, and it's a miracle if they're not. He took a frightful beating. I've often heard that a big goose can hit like a sledgeham-

128

mer with his wings, and now I'm a believer. By the way, Josie, just why are you trying to save this dog's life?"

The question took her by surprise. She stopped and said, "Why, because of moral responsibility, I suppose. I own the geese."

"Good, but not good enough. You have another, better reason, Josie: You've seen the look in your son's eyes. You just can't bear to see him deeply hurt. Right?"

"Yes."

"Do you agree with me that it would be really useless for me to look for the Beagle's collar? I can assure you that he has never worn a collar in his life. To be perfectly blunt, Josie, this is the little pack dog, and you know it as well as I do."

She looked at him for a long moment, then nodded.

"Did you see any other dogs?"

"Just one," she admitted. "He ran into the woods."

"Show me where." He followed her to the point where King had stood. He looked at the dog's tracks in the snow and asked, "A big dog? Black?"

"Yes."

"Let's follow his tracks for a bit." They did, and when they came to the body of the doe, the vet studied all of the dog tracks and said, "There were four of them. Two big ones and two little ones. One of the little ones is a Beagle. I'm sorry, Josie, but because of the deer, this will have to be reported. I'll do it for you, but I think I'll wait until morning. They're predicting a heavy snowfall tonight. Let's hope it covers all of the tracks. Do we have a secret, Josie?"

"We do," she said, and she wanted to kiss him—but he was a balding bachelor, and she didn't want to risk embarrassing him.

"If we succeed in saving this dog, you have a difficult job ahead of you," said the vet as they walked back toward the garage.

"I do?"

"Yes. I'm something of a mind reader, you see, so I knew you would keep the dog. I can assure you that a Beagle makes a wonderful pet for a boy."

They walked along and then Josie stopped and asked, "Are you trying to tell me something?"

"Just that this particular Beagle may never amount to much as a pet, and we don't have to save him. Now hold on, please hear me out! I know a great deal about canine temperament, Josie, and I've never heard of anyone turning a pack dog into a good citizen. Now I'm not saying it would be impossible to reform this one, because he's still a pup and there's always the exception—but I am saying that it will take a good deal more than love and good intentions. It will take patience and understanding and watchfulness and training and an infinite amount of time. And even with all that help, the chances are that this dog will still be a tramp. You read about the human counterpart in the papers every day: The rehabilitated convict who goes on parole and is back in prison the next week. So this is the time, right now, when you must decide. Will it be just a little heartbreak for Henry today, or will you risk a giant-sized heartache for him later on?"

He wouldn't come right out and say it, but he was telling her that he could give the dog another type of shot—one that would put Murphy to sleep forever, and Henry need never know.

Josie understood. The vet had given her his professional opinion, and now the little hound's life was truly in her hands. "I should hate you," she said, and she turned her head away and started to cry.

"I hate myself. It wasn't easy to say those things. It never is."

Josie cried for over a minute, and stopped only after the vet gave her his fresh handkerchief. She dabbed her eyes with the white linen and without a word, started for the garage.

The vet followed her and he was smiling. He knew her decision, for he was something of a mind reader.

Murphy lived.

It was touch and go for the first forty-eight hours and then, on the third day, the pup accepted some liquid nourishment. On the fifth day, when he devoured solid food and looked around for more, the vet took him off the critical list.

And all during that time, Henry and Josie were the dog's chief nurses. Every four hours, one of them spooned medicine down Murphy's throat. The vet showed them just how to do it: One hand held the jaws open and head back; the other spooned the medicine over the tongue as far back as possible; then, the jaws were held shut and the neck stroked.

After a few days, the nurses spilled more of the medicine than the patient consumed. The brown stuff tasted awful to Murphy; and, as his strength returned, he fought every drop of it.

George, as assistant nurse, was on duty at the end and the beginning of each day: Midnight and four in the morning. He grumbled about the four o'clock shift, for he was never fully awake and the medicine that splattered on his bathrobe made permanent stains.

131

The workshop part of the garage was Murphy's hospital ward. Long before his legs grew steady under him, his mind told him that he had never had it so good. He certainly didn't lack for attention or care, and the ward was nice and warm at 65 degrees—for Josie thought the vet's 50 degrees was too cold. The patient's bed—a laundry basket with a pillow as a mattress—was the most comfortable one Murphy had ever known. And while he was alone most of the night, the feeling of loneliness never entered his head: His body required extra sleep, and even when he did awaken he wasn't really alone, for Henry had loaned him a radio and all through the dark hours the beautiful strains of the world's finest symphonies were there to keep him company. Music is as soothing for animals as it is for people.

Two weeks after his defeat in the cornfield, it was apparent that he would, someday, be almost as good as new. A scar on the inside of one foreleg—a gift from the gander—would be his only physical momento, but it would neither detract from his handsomeness nor offend his pride.

The geese knew he was in the garage. They spent the days huddled in front of the closed doors. From time to time, the gander, and a wife or two, would waddle around the building and then rejoin the gaggle. At first, Josie thought they were keeping the enemy surrounded, and then she decided that they were sentries on patrol—guarding the fallen foe against any future danger. She was right, for they were guarding Murphy—as the vet discovered on the day he attempted to enter the garage alone.

That was the day the vet told Josie his services were no longer required. "I'm almost sorry he's doing so well, I enjoy seeing the little fellow. Bring him around in a couple of weeks and we'll give him some preventative shots. Look at him. He's a happy one, that's for sure, and I'd swear his expression spells gratitude."

"Changed your mind about him?" asked Josie.

"Didn't I agree that there's always the exception? I hope this is the one. He certainly doesn't exhibit any wild tendencies, but never underestimate the intelligence of a pack dog. And don't be surprised if he runs away—right out of your lives—the first chance he gets."

"Why, that's a terrible thing to say! This dog appreciates the fact that we saved his life! Don't you believe in anything?"

The vet smiled and said, "I believe that if this dog fails to respond to the conditions he finds here, then no pack dog in the world can ever be reformed. Well, I'm off to deliver a calf. But Josie, please accept this advice in the spirit that it's meant: For the first few weeks outdoors, keep this Beagle on a leash, just in case he has a fond memory or two for the good old days."

"When can we start taking him outdoors?"

"Today, but for no more than a half hour. Add an hour every day and split up the time between morning and afternoon."

Josie passed the information on to Henry when he returned home from school, but she forgot the advice about the leash. Minutes later, when she remembered, she looked out the window and saw Henry walking toward the cornfield. The Beagle was at the boy's left side, just as if he had been trained to heel, and his stern was wagging. Strung out behind them in single file was the gaggle of geese.

It was a lucky thing she forgot about the leash, for Murphy

133

might have considered it a sign of bondage. Still, he didn't seem to resent the collar and license tag George brought home for him to wear. After a few days of trying to scratch the strange things off, he accepted them, for they didn't hamper his eating or his running.

The license tag was as much of a surprise to Henry and Josie as it was to Murphy. George never told his wife or son, but the idea had been inspired by Art Purdy's visit to the lawyer's office.

George was surprised to see Art away from the service station during business hours, and he asked, "You in some sort of trouble, Art?"

"No, this is sort of a social visit, Mr. Deane. Just thought you'd like to know that Henry is the happiest kid in town since you got him that Beagle. Just the right breed, too."

"Thank you, Art."

"Now, I'm not one to stick my nose where it doesn't belong, Mr. Deane, but I'm a little worried about this dog. Quite a few people are saying he's the Beagle who was running around with that pack. You know, the dogs that raised hob at the Poodle kennel and who supposedly frightened the Cat Woman to death. And didn't they find the doe near your place about the time you found your stray? Some people think pack dogs are lions, if you know what I mean!"

"And that worries you, Art?"

"Why, not as much as the sheriff worries me. Now I've known and liked Peter Long most of my life. He may be the best sheriff we've ever had, but he may also be the first one without a sense of humor. I can tell you that he's already taken a lot of kidding about not finding the pack Beagle."

"You can stop worrying, Art. I don't think Peter would take a dog from a boy."

"Not any old dog, Mr. Deane, but this is a special dog. According to county law, a pack dog should be a dead dog. So I hope there won't be any trouble, but don't be surprised if there is. Time I got back to my gas pumps, I guess."

"Thanks for dropping in, Art."

"Well, I've had it on my mind. I don't mind telling you that a Beagle would only join a pack out of necessity, never choice."

Long after Art had gone, the lawyer sat at his desk thinking about all that had been said and implied. Did anyone have the legal right to shelter and protect a pack dog? The moral right, yes, but what about legal?

From the very first, both he and Josie had accepted the fact that the little hound belonged to the pack. And both were well aware of the risk involved—that the dog might turn bad and cause trouble. Neither of them had suspected the greater risk—that the dog could be taken away and shot. In effect, they had been thinking only of Henry's happiness, and all along they had planned on getting a dog for him anyway. Now the boy had his dog, and he loved it. George hated to think of the shattering consequences if the dog were taken away from him.

It's too bad we didn't wait for the Collie, mused George. Who ever heard of a Collie running with a pack? Who ever heard of a Collie silly enough to tangle with a Toulouse gander? Why, his own had never even chased a cat. The Collie was a gentleman, never a rogue.

George sighed and turned to the problem at hand: When is a pack dog not a pack dog? He didn't know. But he did know a great deal about private property rights, and that sort of thinking prompted him to put on his hat and visit the town clerk's office. There he purchased the dog license for the Beagle, designating Henry as the owner. At least it would be something to lean on when and if trouble came. He thought that it might come, and he was right.

⤳ ⤳ ELEVEN ⤳ ⤳

ON ONE DECEMBER DAY, HENRY took two mighty strides toward manhood: He learned to lie with grace, and to tell the truth without fear of consequences.

The lie was told just before the bell rang for algebra class.

"I'm mad at you," said Bess Hawthorne, and she looked mad.

"Why?" asked Henry, in his best tone of innocence. He suspected why.

"Because you promised to help me find my Beagle. You found him, and now you're keeping him for yourself! That's not fair!"

"I didn't find this Beagle, he found me," Henry assured her. "Anyway, this is a different Beagle. Not the one I saw with you. Honest!"

She stared at him, then smiled and said, "Will you come to my birthday party?"

The bell rang, and for the next fifty minutes Henry found it difficult to concentrate on algebra. He was quite pleased with himself. He had lied and Bess believed him. On the other hand, it had not been a common or genuine lie. If a man becomes a soldier and goes to war is he the same man when he comes home and takes off his uniform? Well, the Beagle had been in a war, so was he the same Beagle? Of course not!

After class, Bess asked again, "Will you come to my party?"

"When?"

"Saturday."

"Will I be the only boy?"

"Of course not. There will be seven girls and seven boys, because it's my fourteenth birthday. You'll come?"

"Yes, thank you. What time next Saturday?"

"Who said anything about next Saturday? My birthday is in March."

"Three months from now?"

"Yes. I'm making extravagant preparations. Now don't forget, the first Saturday in March! And Henry, will you still help me find my Beagle?"

He promised, but he considered the promise a way to keep her happy and not a lie. He didn't feel the Beagle was a proper breed for girls anyway. Art Purdy felt the same way.

His great success with the lie influenced his decision to tell the whole truth about the Beagle. When the Deane family sat down to dinner that evening Henry plunged right into his confession: "I have something to tell both of you about our dog."

"Oh, has he learned something new?" asked George. He was still amazed that the Beagle had learned the basic commands so quickly.

"No, this is something else," Henry explained, "something I should have told you earlier, I guess. I hope this won't come as a shock to you, but our Beagle is the one from that wild pack." Henry paused and looked from his father to his mother. They were exchanging smiles, and the boy misunderstood. "I know it's hard to believe, but it's a fact. I thought you would have put two and two together by now, Mom."

"Why?" asked Josie.

"You saw that big black dog in the field that day. He was probably King, the pack leader."

"Why did you wait until now to tell us this?" asked George. The words came out indistinctly for he was trying to sound stern and suppress a chuckle, all at once. So he tried again and put the words another way with, "You should have told us the first day."

"Too risky," Henry told him. "I was afraid you wouldn't let me keep him. What I needed was time, so that he could prove to you that he's not mean or wild. You see, I knew he was as gentle and obedient as any dog, ever."

"You mean you thought he was a good dog," corrected Josie. "How could you really know?"

"Because we were already old friends," Henry confessed. Then he told his parents all about meeting the Beagle at the Cat Woman's, and of the hours they had spent playing together. He also told them how he taught the dog to sit, to come, to heel, and to retrieve a ball.

"Where did the Cat Woman get him?" asked George.

"Oh, he just arrived at her place one day. I suppose he got tired of the pack life and went looking for a home. He was living there when the sheriff saw him. I'm sure he never frightened the old woman. She loved him, although she didn't think he was a dog. She called him a messenger."

139

"Did you ever notice any other dogs around there?" asked Josie.

"No, and I don't think the pack ever came close. Most dogs would consider the place unsafe, with all those cats around. But the Beagle was different. He liked cats and cats liked him. I imagine he came from a good home and was used to cats. I'm almost sure he's housebroken. When can he start living in the house?"

Josie was absolutely sure about the dog's social behavior. The pup had been her constant companion for almost two weeks during Henry's school hours and, in all that time, he did not need correction. Although it was his first real experience in home living, Murphy refrained from chewing rugs and curtains and slippers and took such strange things as the washing machine and vacuum cleaner in his stride. He was now a senior puppy, and so mannerly that he would bark and run to the door when nature called. Even Josie was convinced that he had once lived in a house and had been trained, although that was really not the case. The only other time he barked was when strangers came into the yard or when Josie turned on the television set. She considered him a guard and a born critic.

Josie did not answer Henry's question that night. She waited for George to say something, for he was the head of house—more or less. Finally, he said, "I've been wondering about bringing him into the house, too. I'll discuss the matter later with your mother."

"We'd save money," Henry reminded his father. "We could cut down on the heat in the garage."

Henry was studying in his own room when his parents started to discuss the matter. Josie said that she thought it was high time the dog came into the house and that she was sure it would be no trouble at all to housebreak him.

"I'm not against it, but I don't think we should rush it," said George. "You see, we may be getting into something of a pickle over adopting this dog." Then he told her about Art Purdy's visit, and about the law, and about the local wagging tongues.

"Let them wag!" declared Josie. "This is the gentlest, safest dog I've ever known. Why, he's as harmless as a baby!"

"Now let's not get excited, Josie. Facts are facts, and our Beagle is a pack dog, or an ex-pack dog anyway. We know it and apparently the whole community does, too. Ask yourself this: Would I feel safe if my closest neighbor had a pack dog for a pet, and would I want my children to play with such a dog?"

"George, you are talking like a lawyer!"

"I may be thinking like a lawyer, but I'm talking as a husband and a father and a warden. I'm agreeable to whatever you want to do, Josie. Bring him in if you like. But just consider that it might be wise to wait a bit. If we lose this dog, it will be very hard on Henry, but it will be worse if the dog is a house pet and sleeping in his room."

"George Deane! Do you mean to sit there and tell me that you'd let the law take this dog away from Henry without a fight?"

He was offended and replied, "Was that question necessary?"

She went to him and kissed him, saying, "No, and I'm sorry. The Beagle is very lucky to have such a smart lawyer in the family."

"As the family lawyer, I'm going to propose one thing

141

more, Josie. Only we three members of the Deane family seem to believe that a pack dog can be reformed. This means that we're a nice family, I suppose, but it could also mean that we're a family of fools. I think we have to face the possibility—unlikely as it may seem now—that our Beagle may destroy our faith in him and prove that we really are fools. If that day ever comes, Josie, we'll just have to get rid of him. Does that make sense?"

"The day will never come, but you do make sense. We'll tell Henry tomorrow. I think he should know that we may be in trouble and he should be prepared. But you'd better tell him about that. I might cry."

So Murphy continued to spend his nights in the garage, but he didn't seem to mind. Henry gave him a run about nine-thirty, and George or Josie would do the same two hours later. They also put fresh water in the pan and turned on the radio. The pup was alone, then, until morning, but he slept as soundly as a tired horse, and he developed—subconsciously at least—a fine appreciation of music.

"Will you help me?" asked George one night when he returned from his eleven-thirty visit to Murphy.

"How?" Josie wanted to know.

"Well, I've been putting off writing a note to Brad Simpson. I really should tell him that it doesn't look as though we'll need a Collie pup after all."

"I'll drop him a note tomorrow," Josie volunteered. And she did, but the writing of the note proved more difficult than she had imagined. How do you tell an old Dartmouth grad that your son prefers a pack Beagle to a blue-blooded Collie?

Henry had a far easier time writing a long letter to Jerry Walker. The words just seemed to flow:

142

Well, I finally have my dog, and he's probably the best Beagle in the whole country. Would hate to tell you how much he cost. He is extremely smart and I have had no trouble training him. My mother and father are very impressed with his intelligence, and Mr. Purdy, who is an expert on hounds, says he is outstanding. [On the fifth page, the boy just couldn't resist taking a mild poke at his friend in the city:] He's still a pup, but next year he'll be ready for hunting—he has all the instincts right now. You should see him with his nose to the ground when we're in the woods. Here, all the fellows our age have guns and go hunting. If your parents don't think it's too dangerous, maybe you can visit and go hunting with me. [Henry was so full of spirit that he added a postscript:] The girls here are more natural. Not silly like Grace and some others I could name. When you visit, you will see what I mean. Bess, who is my steady, more or less, is a keen dancer and very beautiful, and doesn't talk all the time.

Art Purdy proved to be an excellent judge of character and an even better prophet. The constant references to the pack Beagle finally got under the sheriff's skin; some of the talk was in jest, but a good deal of it came to his ears as complaints. Peter Long was a proud man and he knew his duty. The law was always right, and he was paid to uphold the law; he had never made an exception in his life. He was the best sheriff Green Valley had ever had.

He had all the evidence he needed, circumstantial and otherwise, and he could have marched right in and seized Murphy, but he respected a person's feelings. When he walked into George Deane's office, he was prepared to make things go as easily as possible for all concerned.

"My brother lives up around Syracuse and he sent me this," said Peter as he handed George a snapshot. "Breeds

Beagles as a hobby. Fine looking litter, wouldn't you say?"

"I would," agreed George, "and I'd also say that I can't tell one pup from another. Identical septuplets. Amazing. How old are they?" He thought he knew why the sheriff was there, but the snapshot puzzled him.

"Ten weeks about, and from the best bloodlines. I guess you know why I'm here, George. What I had in mind was sort of an exchange. I'd be happy to give Henry one of those pups. He could take his pick."

They were sitting on opposite sides of the desk. George leaned forward and said, "That's very kind and thoughtful of you, Peter, but it just wouldn't work. Boys love dogs, but just one at a time. They can't fall out of love quickly, and it's impossible for them to transfer it."

"Hadn't thought of that. You know, it's the same way with grown men. To tell the truth, I'd like another Setter, but there'll never be another one like my Sport." Peter shook his head before continuing, "Well, you can't say I didn't try to make this easy for the boy."

"I appreciate that, Peter. Now where do we go from here?"

"This is the law and nothing personal, George, but you're going to have to hand that Beagle over to me."

"Isn't there a law that says one is innocent until proven guilty?"

"Yes, and unfortunately it's just for people. Anyway, I've seen him in your yard a few times and I can prove he's not innocent. He's the same hound who came for me at the Cat Woman's place."

"Which proves absolutely nothing. But do you know what I can prove? That he belonged to her, Peter, and that he couldn't possibly have frightened her, and that he was sim-

144

ply protecting her property. What you need is professional advice. You have circumstantial evidence, Peter, and I can shoot it full of holes. It would never stand up in court."

Peter blushed and got to his feet. "I wanted to handle this in friendly fashion, George, but you sound like you're going to fight me."

"I'm not fighting you, Peter. I'm fighting for a dog's life."

"Well, I don't mind telling you that I'm very surprised! Thought until this minute that all lawyers were level-headed. How are you going to fight positive identification? I'm not the only one, you know. There's the whole Wilson family and Thad Taylor, too!"

The men stared at each other. Peter was waiting for an answer, and when it came it was in the form of a question: "Are you willing to entertain a suggestion?"

"Why, that depends. What do you have in mind?" asked the sheriff.

"A compromise that would work in your favor. If this dog is a criminal, Peter, the world has never known a more friendly or harmless one. So I'm suggesting the granting of time. I give you my word: If the dog ever turns bad, if I even suspect him of turning bad, I'll hand him over to you. Henry would understand that. What do you say, Peter?"

"You want me to stand by and wait until this innocent little pack dog chews off some kid's arm? Don't you know anything at all about pack dogs? I don't care what they seem to be, every damn one is smarter than you and me put together! Sure he's acting sweet right now, but what does he have to lose? No!"

"Damn it all, George, you're trying to make me feel like a criminal. I'm just doing my duty!"

"Would you mind telling me when you plan to pick up the dog?"

"I'm in no hurry. Whenever it's convenient for you. Just don't lose the Beagle. Maybe you and your wife can figure out some way to tell your boy. Phone me when you're ready."

Peter left the office. George locked his arms behind his head and leaned back in the swivel chair. He stared at the ceiling for several minutes, thinking about his bold promise to fight for the dog, and about what an impossible fight it would be in the face of positive identification. Then he leaned forward and was about to stand up when he noticed the snapshot of the seven puppies. It was still on his desk blotter.

He picked up the snapshot and studied it, and again he was impressed by the similarity of all the pups. Then he saw that the markings were not really identical, but certainly close enough to cause confusion.

He stood up and walked to the window. The snapshot in his hand was the key to his defense strategy, and new thoughts were whirring in his mind.

He stood there looking out of the window, and after awhile he realized that his eyes were fastened on Art Purdy's service station. The lawyer smiled. The strategy was beginning to take shape. The defense of his new client, the pack Beagle, would begin with Art Purdy, the Beagle authority.

George Deane reached for his hat. Then he crossed to the wall mirror and faced it. "You're a good, clever, crooked lawyer," he said to his reflection. "Yes, you are!"

Art Purdy was reading a hunting magazine when the lawyer walked into the office. "Sorry," said Art, "didn't hear you drive in."

146

"Don't get up. I walked over. I'm just looking for a little information."

"You came to the right man. I'm full of all sorts of information and I don't guarantee any of it."

"Art, how many times have you seen Henry's Beagle?"

"Four or five times, I'd say. That I can guarantee. Why?"

"I was just wondering how he compared with your own dogs."

"Well, now, I'd swear he was from the same line breeding. Even looks like my hounds. I've got a half dozen that could be cousins. Same size, heads and ear sets. Pretty close markings, too."

"Identical?"

"Oh, I wouldn't say that, but close enough so's I'd take a second look—if Henry's dog was running around with mine. Why?"

"I'm thinking as you're talking, Art. You might be able to help me with a little problem. Tell me, is there anyone around here who knows more about Beagles than you?"

"Of course not! Who's been lying to you?"

"Not a soul. Just wanted to make sure."

"Let me tell you, Mr. Deane, I've been breeding, raising and training Beagles for close to fifty years. Proud of it, too. Know everything about the breed. Ever hear of a five inch Beagle? Plenty of five inchers in England a century ago. The lords and ladies loved them."

"I recognize you as Green Valley's authority," chuckled George.

"Well, now, I'm not so modest. I consider myself the highest ranking authority in the state!"

"Art, you said that you've seen Henry's Beagle four or five times. Would you know him again anywhere, anytime? Sup-

147

pose you went to California next month and a Beagle came running down the street. You've had a long, good look at this Beagle, understand? He reminds you of Henry's dog. Would it be possible for you to be absolutely sure that it was not Henry's dog?"

Art frowned and rubbed his chin before replying, "For a lawyer, you are pretty uninformed. You know how many Beagles there are in this country? Close to four million! You know how many look alike? Exactly alike? Thousands of them. Same heads, ears, eyes, tails, expressions, markings. Oh, when I see this dog in California, I might say he was Henry's and I might not. But either way, if he closely resembled Henry's, I couldn't be absolutely sure. You'd have to know the dog real well to be sure. As I said before, at first glance I might confuse Henry's dog with some of my own. And I'm an expert." He noticed that the lawyer was studying the calendar on the wall. "This is Thursday, in case you're wondering."

"Yes, I know," said George. He looked at Art and smiled. "You said you wanted some information?"

"Yes, and you've been giving it to me," George assured him. "Now I'm going to ask you for some material help, too, Art, but I'll understand if you don't want to go along with me." Then he told Art about the sheriff's visit, and of all that had been said, and of his own decision to save the Beagle's life, if it were possible to do so. "As I see it," he explained, "the dog has one slim chance: Can the witnesses positively identify him as the pack Beagle? They are all sure they can. And I'm sure they'll be able to do so—if they are asked to see and identify just this one dog. But suppose I challenge the witnesses? Suppose I ask them to identify one Beagle from a group of similarly marked Beagles. What then, Art?"

148

Art Purdy was grinning from ear to ear. "Just tell me where and when," he promised, "and I'll be there with a half dozen of my dogs! Matter of fact, I'll make a few phone calls and round up another dozen Beagles. We might as well turn this into a first class show!"

They decided on Saturday morning at ten. Art promised to get the dogs to the Deane place a little early. George thanked him, then headed back to his office. Later he would tell Josie and Henry of the sheriff's visit and about the plan of action on Saturday. Then he would phone the sheriff and issue an invitation to a positive identification party. He felt much better. If Art Purdy could deliver a dozen Beagles or so, Henry's dog had an excellent chance for survival.

The lawyer underestimated Art Purdy's devotion to the breed. Within the hour, Art started phoning fellow members of the Tri-County Beagle Club of America. He started right at the top with a call to the president of the club, Justice Rodney H. Blackstone, Supreme Court, New York State.

The sheriff was agreeable. He assured George that he and his witnesses would be at the Deane place at ten sharp on Saturday morning. He also wondered if George wasn't being a little rough on his son, but withheld comment. If the whole thing was handled the right way, Henry would learn a fine moral lesson that would come in handy all of his life: One can't be too careful when choosing one's associates—animal or human.

Peter was supremely confident of the end result. He phoned Sam Hawthorne and told him to be at the Deane place at ten-thirty on Saturday, and to bring along a dog crate. "Now don't be late, Sam, and don't hang around after

I give you the Beagle. Just take off and get him directly to the pound. They'll know what to do with him."

Then the sheriff visited Thad Taylor and asked him to be present.

"Count me out," said Thad. "I do better than thirty percent of my week's business on Saturday morning."

"Why, it'll only take a few minutes, Thad. You'd be doing your duty as a citizen."

"I'm doing my duty by trying to make enough money to pay taxes."

So Peter tried the sentimental approach: "Wasn't the Cat Woman one of your best customers? Don't you sort of owe this to her?"

"Yes, but on the other hand, Mrs. Deane is one of my best living customers. She's not at all like some people I could mention, who drive twenty miles to the supermarket to save two cents on bacon; although your wife doesn't do that every week. No, Peter, I couldn't care less if this is the pack Beagle or not. I don't care if I never see another dog in my life."

But Mrs. Wilson, the Poodle lady, was very cooperative. "I'll be there," she promised, "and you can count on Sally and my husband, too. Once a vicious dog, always a vicious dog. Temperament is built-in through generations of breeding, and who can say what's behind this dog's breeding? I sometimes think that the American Kennel Club should license all breeders. There are just too many irresponsible people breeding dogs in this country. Breeding is really a science, you see."

"You're pretty sure that you can identify him, if this is the same Beagle?"

"Oh, yes. Now the thing to look for first is that sore he car-

150

ried high on the right thigh. The coat will have grown back by now, but it will still be a little different on that spot."

"I hadn't thought of that."

"Well, of course, you're not a breeder."

So the sheriff really didn't need Thad, and his confidence never waned. He retired early on Friday night, telling himself that he could use a good night's sleep, for the day ahead would be a difficult one. Not just the Deane affair, but all sorts of odds and ends that he'd allowed to accumulate. As far as the boy and the dog were concerned, the sheriff's own conscience was absolutely clear.

That's what he told himself, but he couldn't understand why sleep didn't come.

❧❧ ❧❧ TWELVE ❧❧ ❧❧

KING AWAKENED SHORTLY after dawn. Rover and Mutt were huddled together on the bare ground nearby. They were still asleep, and the black dog wondered if he could steal away for a few minutes and take care of his thirst. He wanted to be by himself, too, for he was losing patience with Mutt. The only time the little mongrel was really quiet was when he was asleep. He had plenty of spirit and courage, but King often wished that Mutt would get himself lost.

The mongrel could never take the place of Murphy. King was sure the Beagle was dead. If the big, fat hens with the strange necks hadn't killed his little friend that day, certainly the boy with the gun did. King had been sullen ever since, and several times he had turned on the uncomplaining Rover for no reason.

The big black dog crawled on his belly until he was out from under the cottage. He noted that it was not snowing,

153

and that was all to the good, for plenty of snow already covered the ground. It was deeper than he had ever known; and, for the first time in his life, he resented it. The small game had all but disappeared; livestock and poultry lived behind closed doors; even rabbit hutches had wooden barriers; and, if it had not been for a few weakened, starving deer, he and his pack would now be suffering the acute pains of hunger. But the lack of abundant food was only part of the problem; men with guns had visited the lake in recent weeks and, although they didn't do any shooting, King suspected they were looking for him. But each time he saw them first and did not wait to find an answer.

As he started off for the nearby stream, Mutt barked somewhere behind him. The black dog stopped and waited; and, as Mutt approached, he wheeled and snarled and chased the mongrel back to the cottage. Mutt dove under the house and stayed there.

Again, King headed for the frozen stream. He found the ice thin near the edge of a boulder, broke through it with several thumps of his huge paw, then stuck his muzzle into the hole to lap the cold water. Ice formed on his whiskers almost as soon as he lifted his head. A gray squirrel scolded him, and a blue jay added screeching insults, but King did not look up. He was not interested in mere snacks—and he couldn't climb a tree.

He could think more clearly now. The pack's last square meal had been three days before at the county dump. The garbage trucks unloaded their treasures there almost every day, and a dog could select from a wide range of dishes. But King disliked the dump, for he found the smells offensive and the society there—cats and rats and even amateur pack dogs—was not to his liking. Besides, Mutt had gorged everything in sight, with no thought of selectivity, and he was still complaining.

The time had come for King to take the lead. The pack was hungry. As he walked back to the cottage, he thought about the likeliest places to find something as satisfactory as a fat hen. Fat hen? The lovely thought brought him to a halt. With snow on the ground, fat hens were safe in their houses. But there had been snow on the ground at that place near the cliff on the day that Murphy died—and big, fat ᴧens with long necks had been all over the place. Were they still there?

It would be easy enough to find out. A scouting trip would provide the answer.

The black dog decided it would be best to scout alone. Mutt might yapp, and that would be too risky in broad daylight.

Rover and Mutt would just have to wait under the cottage until he returned. They'd be safe there.

King trotted off to the cliff overlooking the Deane place.

At nine o'clock on that Saturday morning, Art Purdy phoned George Deane that a friend was on his way over with a few dogs. When George passed on the information to Josie, she asked, "Did he mention the name of the friend?"

"Yes. Rod Blackstone."

"Oh. I thought it might be somebody from around here."

"Art didn't say where he was from. What's that noise? What's going on in the basement?"

"Now, don't get excited. I asked Henry to drive the geese into the basement. We don't want them loose with strange people and strange dogs around."

155

George nodded in agreement. He was really thinking about the surname, Blackstone. "Hold everything," he said. "That name Blackstone does ring a bell. Justice Rodney H. Blackstone of the Supreme Court of New York State. This Rod may be his son! Wouldn't that be something?"

When a station wagon parked in his yard a few minutes later, George hurried outside to greet Art's friend and came close to losing his power of speech. He recognized the friend as Justice Blackstone, in person.

"Wanted to get here early so that we could plan proper strategy," explained Blackstone. "My crates hold six Beagles, and all should closely resemble your pet, if Art's verbal description is accurate. Now then, where is this sheriff-intimidating hound of yours?"

Murphy staged one of the finest welcoming acts of his career. He had never wagged his tail quite so violently, nor licked the hand of a stranger with such warm enthusiasm. It was as if he realized the extreme importance of this particular first impression.

All of the Deanes were pleased to hear Justice Blackstone's appraisal of Murphy: "A true Beagle, end to end. I would say from his ear set that he carries Rowett blood. A merry temperament, and that's certainly typical of the breed. I have the honor of owning a portrait of Edward III, Fourteenth Century. He had his portrait painted with one of his royal hounds. This one is a carbon copy. Well, now, you have a very good dog here. Worth saving."

"What sort of blood did you say he has?" asked Henry.

"Rowett, and that's the very best. All the great ones carried it. Warrior and Pilot and Dolly, for example."

"Did you own those dogs?"

156

"No, young man. I may look over a hundred years old, but I'm not."

Then Henry, with the impatience of youth, asked the question that was foremost in the mind of his parents: "Do you think, sir, that a bad dog can become a good dog?"

Justice Blackstone leaned against his car and studied the Beagle. Murphy sat down and looked up at him. To the observing Deanes, man and dog appeared to be communicating in some mysterious way. "A good and fair question," Justice Blackstone finally said, "and one which I have no intention of answering. I'm willing to observe, on the other hand, that we are really concerned with this dog's present and future, and not his past. What counts is what he is at the moment, and what you will help him to be in all his tomorrows. Now, here is what I have in mind for the meeting with the sheriff and his party."

He had given the matter serious consideration, he said, and felt that in fairness to all concerned, the witnesses should be given every opportunity to identify the Beagle as the pack dog. He wanted a positive identification from each witness. Did all agree?

"I thought we would confuse the witnesses," said George.

"Oh, we will, but not in the beginning," explained the visitor. "Once we get positive identification, we'll have your dog mix freely with the other hounds, and then we'll ask our cocksure witnesses to pick your dog from the group. My thought is to get them out on a limb, and then to saw the limb off. When I was in practice, I considered confident witnesses duck soup. I believe you were a trial lawyer at one time, Mr. Deane?"

George laughed and agreed to the plan. "You brought

157

six dogs, and Art Purdy's bringing another five or six, so we'll have a dozen Beagles for the grand climax. That should be more than enough."

"Oh, no, that won't be nearly enough," said Justice Blackstone. "Several other club members and their dogs will be along shortly. We'll want to get them all out of sight before the sheriff arrives."

"How many more dogs are coming?" asked Josie.

"The honor of the Beagle is close to the heart of every member of the Tri-County Beagle Club of America, Mrs. Deane. I think we can count on at least seventy more Beagles."

"Here they come and right on time," announced Henry. He was looking out the kitchen window as the sheriff and the Wilsons drove into the yard. Those who heard him were his parents, their distinguished visitor, and Murphy.

"The sheriff is bound to ask about all those station wagons," said George.

"Let me handle the explanation if it's needed," suggested Justice Blackstone. "Oh, by the way, it would be best to introduce me as Mister Blackstone, don't you think? I'm off duty and unfrocked, so to speak, and I think I can play my role better as an average taxpayer. Any questions?"

"No, Your Honor," George chuckled.

"Now Henry, you are to remain in here with your dog while your parents and I greet the sheriff's party and arrange rules for this hearing. But stay at your post, and when your father waves, bring this Beagle outside. Immediately. Any questions?"

"No, Sir!"

"As for you, young fellow," continued the justice as he patted Murphy's head, "just be merry and true to your breed." Then he walked to the door, opened it and bowed. "You first, Mrs. Deane."

Josie, George and Justice Blackstone went outside to join the sheriff's party. Sure enough, as soon as George had completed the introductions, the sheriff commented, "Looks like you have quite a bit of company here today, George."

"Unexpected company," explained the justice. "My Club is on its way to a field trial in Maryland, and since we were passing by we thought we'd drop in and discuss a legal matter with George. Defamation of character suit, but it can wait. The others are up in the field exercising their dogs. Just go right ahead, don't mind me."

"I don't know quite how to go about this, Peter," said George Deane, "so suppose you take over."

"Well, as you know, we came here to see if we could identify your Beagle as the pack Beagle. So first of all, we'll need your Beagle."

"Sounds reasonable," said George. He turned and waved, and a few seconds later Henry and Murphy bounded out of the house. The dog ran straight up to the witnesses and played the role of host to perfection, trotting from one to the other, wagging his tail and wiggling his entire body. Then he forgot the adults and paid particular attention to Sally Wilson.

The little girl laughed and dropped to her knees and hugged him. "Is this the one I'm supposed to positively identify?" she asked. "I've never seen this one before. The one who chased me was very mean and twice as big! A little dog like this doesn't scare me."

"That's quite enough, Sally!" said her mother. "This is a

very serious matter, and if the sheriff wants your opinion, he'll ask for it."

"May we have your opinion first, Mrs. Wilson?" asked the sheriff. "Is this the Beagle you saw at your place with the pack?"

"I want a closer look," she said. Then she crouched down and studied Murphy's head at close range, and received a wet lick on her nose. Next she ran her fingers over Murphy's right thigh and announced, "This is new coat. You can almost see the outline where it covers an old wound."

"He has new coat in a dozen other places, too," offered Henry. "On the left thigh, too. He had plenty of big cuts."

Mrs. Wilson was confused by his remarks, but not for long. She stood up and walked around Murphy, and studied him from a score of angles. "Yes," she decided, "this is the pack Beagle."

"Well now, that just confirms my own opinion," said Peter Long. "Same size and same markings as the one that tried to attack me. I'd know him anywhere. What about you, Mr. Wilson?"

The man walked to Murphy's rear and took one more good look at the dog. "This is the one I tried to shoot," he said. "Had him lined up straight in my sights. Still don't know how I missed. Yes, this has to be the one!"

"Well, George, there you are," said Peter Long. "Sorry to put you and your family through all this, but you made the request. You insisted on positive identification, and now you have it."

No one said anything. They all looked at Murphy. The little hound trotted over to Henry and sat, leaning against the boy's leg. For no reason that he could fathom, the dog

160

felt a sudden need for reassurance. Henry patted him gently.

Sally tugged on her mother's skirt and said, "You're wrong, he's much too little."

"Stop it and don't say another word," scolded her mother.

Justice Blackstone smiled and said, "What a charming little girl, Mrs. Wilson." Then he turned to Peter, saying, "Now this is none of my business, sheriff, and I hope you'll pardon a silly question from a dog lover, but does positive identification mean the same to all of us? For instance, does it mean that it would be impossible for you to confuse this Beagle with any other Beagle? Oh, let's say you had to pick him out of a police lineup of ten or twelve Beagles. Could you do it?"

"Every time," said the sheriff. "You must understand, Mr. Blackstone, that I'm trained for this sort of thing. If a man attacks me in broad daylight, I never forget him, and that's happened several times. Now this is the only Beagle who ever came for me, and there's not the slightest chance I'd ever confuse him with another."

"Well, that's amazing," said the justice. "To the layman, one Beagle often looks pretty much like another. One sees so many Beagles, if you know what I mean?"

Mrs. Wilson could not refrain from spreading her own knowledge of canines. "Dogs of the same breed can never really be identical," she explained. "Just as no two sets of human fingerprints are ever identical, so it is with dogs. It's a matter of genetics, of course."

"Thank you! Are you a biologist, Mrs. Wilson?"

"Mrs. Wilson breeds Poodles," Peter informed him. "She has some of the best ones in the country, and she's an authority on dogs in general." The lady beamed her gratitude.

161

"Well, one learns something new every day," said the justice, "but I'm still amazed that you can be so positive about one little dog. Just for the fun of it, why don't we try the police lineup?" He scooped up Murphy on the final words and dashed across the yard in the direction of the cornfield. "Follow me!" he shouted.

His action surprised the witnesses.

"What's that old bird trying to pull here, George?" demanded Peter.

"Now don't get excited, Peter. You heard what he said. He simply wants you to identify our Beagle in a police lineup of Beagles. There are a few more up in the field."

"Just who does he think he is? Why, the man is crazy! He's interfering with the law!"

"Now, Peter, I'm sorry you said that," George told him, his tone very solemn. "And I want to remind all of you here that you are witnesses to Peter's accusation that Mr. Blackstone is crazy. In so doing, he has willfully and deliberately defamed Mr. Blackstone. Further, he has recklessly and maliciously challenged the very integrity of the Supreme Court of this state. And now, Peter, to answer your question about who Mr. Blackstone thinks he is—he thinks he is Justice Rodney H. Blackstone of the Supreme Court. And if there is any doubt about that in your mind, I positively identify him as such."

Silence.

The sheriff recovered first: "I didn't suspect you'd go this far, George, but you're not dealing with a bunch of idiots. We'd know this dog of yours anywhere, and we accept the challenge. Let's go, folks."

He started for the field, and the Poodle lady and her family went with him. Henry wanted to go along, but George restrained his son. "No, we're staying here. The dog might come to us and give himself away."

In the cornfield, the sheriff's party found eighty-four Beagles awaiting them. "Well, here we are and thank you for coming," said Justice Blackstone, welcoming the positive-identifiers. "I'll admit that this is pretty big for a police lineup, but after all, a life is at stake. Now take your time and don't hurry. We still have about seven hours of daylight."

Sally Wilson didn't understand. The little girl jumped up and down and clapped her hands. "I positively identify all of them!" she shouted. "They're all Beagles and this is a Beagle circus!" Her parents were too stunned to pay attention, and soon the little girl was running around with the dogs and trying to pet them all. Then one of them stole her mitten, and she chased the thief.

"If you need a little help," offered Justice Blackstone, "I can tell you that every dog in this field except the Deane one carries an identifying tattoo. Of course, it would not be fair for you to inspect them."

Not a single member of the witness party thanked him.

"I do wish they'd stand still," said Mrs. Wilson. "I'm sure he's one of nine."

Peter was mad and determined. His trained eyes roamed the field, and then he pointed and said, "That one! He's the little one in the group of three right over there!"

"Positive?" asked the justice.

Peter nodded. Then he and the justice crossed to the trio for a close look.

They were still twenty feet from the dogs when Peter wheeled and hurried back to the Wilsons. He was madder than ever and his cheeks turned red. The little dog he'd had his eye on was a carbon copy of the Deane dog, but he'd noticed that it was a bitch.

Peter muttered something to the Wilsons; then they followed him back to the yard. Sam Hawthorne, with his empty crate, was waiting there for him, but Peter walked right past Sam.

"Where's the dog?" called Sam.

Peter climbed into his car, started the motor, and drove off.

"Now just what got into him?" asked Sam.

"The legal term for it is reasonable doubt," explained George. "You can't hang a man just because he resembles a criminal."

The Wilsons were just about to drive off in their car when they discovered that Sally was missing. Henry volunteered to fetch her. It took several minutes, because she didn't want to leave all the Beagles, but finally he returned with her. When the little girl stepped into the car, she said, "When I grow up, I'm not going to breed Poodles. I know what breed I'm going to breed!"

Up in the cornfield, Justice Blackstone advised his club members to round up their dogs. "And be sure you don't take any of mine, and be very sure you don't take the one that's not tattooed." Then, just to be on the safe side, he added, "In other words, make positive identifications of your own hounds."

All during the Beagle circus, King had been crouched behind a rock on the cliff, and he had never been so bewildered. He had been watching the dogs—more than he had ever seen at one time, and every one of them was his friend, Murphy.

So Murphy was alive! And what a miracle Murphy had wrought! What a pack!

The leader forgot about his hunger, forgot about the fat hens. He had rescue on his mind. It would take some doing, but it could be done. Night would be the best time.

King waited until the cornfield was empty; then he started back to the lake. He was feeling much better, already anticipating the reunion with Murphy.

⅔⅓ ⅔⅓ THIRTEEN ⅔⅓ ⅔⅓

IT WAS MURPHY'S FINEST hour—that time in the cornfield
when he won his right to live—with no effort at all on his
part. He would soon forget it, but the Deane family wouldn't
forget it, and Art Purdy wouldn't let anyone in Green Valley
forget it. In no time at all, Art's retelling of the tale would in-
clude two hundred Beagles, and Peter Long would force a
grin and say, "Looked like ten thousand to me." It seemed to
Art that Peter might have a sense of humor after all.

Henry would always remember the day with special pride,
for his Beagle was the only one in the whole world to hold
an honorary pack membership in the Tri-County Beagle
Club of America. The honor was bestowed in a special ceremony before the club's departure, and Justice Blackstone
filled the air with brilliant oratory as he announced the important decision of the club's board of directors.

Within the week, a scroll arrived testifying to Murphy's

honorary membership. Since Murphy still didn't have a name, the scroll gave him a name: Henry Deane's Beagle (Dog). The scroll was framed and hung on the wall in Henry's room, where the boy and Murphy could admire it at will.

The little hound was completely happy—happier even than he had been at the Cat Woman's—for now he was truly a member of a family. He was living, full-time, in the Deane house, and he slept in Henry's room. It didn't take him long to discover that his special bed—the laundry basket with a pillow—was not nearly as comfortable as Henry's bed.

Josie always awakened Henry, and the first few mornings she discovered the dog in bed with him. She scolded Murphy each time and put him on his own bed, saying, "You are to sleep here and nowhere else, understand?"

Finally Murphy understood, and after that she found the dog sound asleep in his basket. She never knew that he listened for her steps on the stairs and, when he heard them, he jumped from Henry's bed to his own.

It took him almost a week to understand that he was to sleep in Henry's room. The nights didn't start out that way! First Henry went to bed, but Murphy stayed downstairs; just before they retired, either Josie or George took him outside for a final run; once back in the house, the dog was led upstairs to Henry's room, where he would sleep until morning. This system saved one unnecessary trip for the parents, but Murphy looked at it another way: While he waited to join Henry, he had time to cultivate his friendship with George. As Josie often observed, "He's a man's dog. When you and Henry are around, he pays absolutely no attention to me." It wasn't a complaint. It was a fact, and she didn't mind.

If it made any sense, or if it were possible, Josie would

have paid Murphy a salary to remain just as he was. Since his coming, the whole atmosphere of the Deane family had changed for the better. Caring for a dog of his own had somehow brought the real Henry to the surface. He was happier and livelier now—far less reticent and far more talkative. The phone rang more often for him, and the caller wasn't always Bess. Although all Josie ever overheard was talk about homework, even that was an indication that he was making friends where there had been none before. And a birthday party was coming up in March! Josie just knew it was the start of a brilliant social career for her son in Green Valley.

She thought that the change was less obvious in George's case, but it was there. His clever defense of the Beagle had amounted to far more than a fight for the dog's life—it had been stuffy George's open declaration of love for his son. And George had become a hero to his boy—boy and man were drawn closer together. It was simple for Josie to substantiate that fact: Who would have dreamed that the boy would go ice fishing with his father, and who would have believed that Henry would listen and even ask questions as George retold his worn tales of his football days at Dartmouth—especially the one about the time he fell on the ball behind the Princeton line, although the record book insisted that Dartmouth hadn't scored that year. Well, Josie wouldn't have believed it months ago, but she believed it now.

If Murphy was happy, so were all the Deanes. Henry's birthday was just four days away, and Christmas was two days later. The boy had insisted that the dog was more than enough for both events, and he wanted no additional gifts. He was sincere, and he was also trying to save his parents' money, but there would be gifts: An expensive fly rod and reel for his birthday, a rifle and skis for his Christmas—all

George's ideas. George had already purchased a Christmas gift for the Beagle: A real dog bed with a cedar-stuffed mattress, which Murphy would rarely use.

"I do want one gift for Christmas," Henry finally admitted. "Or maybe it's a privilege. We still keep calling our Beagle just 'Dog' or 'Pup' or 'Hey You.' I've selected a name for him."

"The privilege is hereby granted," said George as head of the family. "What's the name?"

"Kris," said Henry. "Kris with a K. Kris for Christmas, but we can't start calling him that until Christmas Day."

Murphy was present, and he thumped his tail on the floor each time Henry said the name. The boy suspected that the dog knew the name was for him, and that it wouldn't be a surprise gift after all.

"I think he knows it's his name already," Henry whispered. "So let's not say it again. He may forget by Christmas."

Murphy didn't thump his tail that time. He was asleep.

But later that night, when they were in bed and the lights were out, Josie knew it was safe to mention the name again. "Kris is a very cute name for the dog, don't you think? It fits him."

"Yes," agreed George. "It's short and he's small."

He expected her to laugh, but all she said was, "Listen!"

"To what?"

"Listen, there it is again!"

"I don't hear anything."

"You will if you listen." She waited a few moments, then said, "I heard a dog barking, 'way out back, over near the cliff, I think. Strange."

"What's so strange about a barking dog?"

"Oh, weeks ago—it must have been before we found the Beagle, I think—I was out in the cornfield with the geese and

170

I heard the same sharp bark. I looked but I didn't see anything, and I didn't hear it again that day. Listen! There it is again!"

"Don't hear a thing," said George. "Goodnight, Josie."

She stayed awake and listened. She heard George's steady breathing and knew he was asleep, and then she heard the sharp bark again. Very carefully, so as not to awaken George, Josie slipped out of bed and went to the window. It was a black night, and she couldn't see ten feet ahead much less all the way to the cliff. Then she reached to her dresser and found the flashlight. She pointed its strong beam out the window. All she saw was falling snow. It was a ridiculous thing to do, and she was glad George was sound asleep. He would have laughed.

Up on the cliff, King saw the flicker of light and was bitterly disappointed. He and Rover were having a tough time trying to keep Mutt quiet, and now the little mongrel had spoiled everything. Silence is an important part of a rescue operation.

King turned to Mutt and growled his disapproval. The rescue of Murphy would have to await another night.

Josie didn't hear the sharp barks on the next few nights, and finally she forgot all about them. She and George stayed up later than usual, for Christmas was closing in on them and there were still cards to address and presents to wrap and cookies and cakes to prepare. If there was one Deane family tradition George insisted upon, it was home-baking for the Christmas table: Stollen, brandied fruit cake, plum pudding, Scotch shortbread, mince and pumpkin pies, sand tortes, and George's favorite pfeffernüsse cookies.

Josie was willing, and often the baking was done late at night.

Then came the night when the house was black.

It was the pack's third visit of the week, but things looked more promising to King: No lights up front; no sign of people; and fair vision—thanks to the moon and the snow. Even Mutt kept his mouth shut for a change! Conditions seemed ideal for the rescue of Murphy. The big black dog was confident that he would find the Beagle and he wasn't concerned about reaching him. The necessary steps would be taken as soon as the little hound was located. If only Mutt would continue to keep his big mouth shut!

The leader turned and snarled at Mutt. That sometimes worked. Then he stepped over to Rover and gave the yellow dog a meaningful look. Rover stared back at him and grunted—as if in acceptance of orders.

They were in the field, about a hundred yards from the house. King led the way, with Rover well behind him and Mutt far to the rear. The snow was almost up to the leader's shoulders, and he plowed through it slowly, one deliberate step after another. His route to the yard was in an arc, designed to bring the pack behind the garage, since the building would shield the pack's approach from the dark house. Lights or no lights, a house was a house and always a menace.

King stopped when he reached the garage and looked back. He could see Rover, but not Mutt. He almost hoped that Mutt was lost. As he looked, Rover stopped in his tracks. The yellow dog was acting according to plan.

Satisfied that all was well, the black dog worked his way toward the yard, hugging the side of the garage. Then he stopped short, for a scent had reached his nostrils. The scent of hen. He proceeded very cautiously and inched his head around the corner of the building. There, on the packed snow, was a round puff of feathers. Ah, one of those well remembered big, fat hens. He studied her. She didn't seem to have a head.

The sleeping, female Toulouse had retired early. The rest of the gaggle had not been ready to settle down, and she had assumed that they would join her when they were. But Walter Mitty and his harem had bedded on the far side of the house. Geese need no shelter and are not particular about sleeping quarters, needing only a barrier against the wind.

For the moment, King forgot about Murphy. It was Christmas Eve, but the black dog would have considered the hen a gift meant for him at any time. She was only ten feet away. A simple matter—even simpler, if he could figure out where her head was. Well, he couldn't afford to wait. He'd just grab, and if she had a head, he'd take care of that soon enough. Quite a mouthful, but his jaws were ample for the task.

Six quick steps and a leap would do it. He tensed his muscles and moved for the kill, just as Mutt barked to his rear. The black dog slipped on the packed, icy snow, and his body slammed into the goose. His one hundred and fifty pounds sent her sprawling a distance of ten feet, and she squawked every inch of the way. Now he saw that she had a head and a long neck, too. He turned and leaped for her, and something very sharp banged into his nose. His responding shriek was almost human. The pain was sharp and it infuriated him. He dove again, snarling and slashing, and a mighty wing thumped down on his good ear.

The hen that was not a hen worked furiously, concentrating on her assailant's head. She did not see Rover until it was too late. His jaws found one of her legs. She twisted and turned on him, exposing her neck to King. His teeth found her low on the neck, and he held on as she thrashed and squawked through her final moments.

A dog was barking. It seemed to King that the barks came from the house, and the sounds were familiar ones. So that's where Murphy was! He looked at Rover, but the yellow dog was already dining on his prize. So King advanced alone toward the house.

Then Mutt was at his rear, barking his fool head off, and blurred forms were rushing directly at him. Walter Mitty and his harem were charging the invaders, and the pack dogs had never known such vicious, angry hens.

Glass shattered and a light appeared upstairs in the house, but King was much too busy to hear or notice. He and Rover had been outnumbered before, but never by long-necked warriors with secret weapons.

Mutt dashed back and forth on the fringes of the action, keeping a safe distance. He was sure that all he had to do was bark up a victory. He was wrong.

The house was dark that night because Henry was alone. His parents had left about nine o'clock to join in the Christmas caroling. The boy had remained at home to wrap his Christmas presents. He had completed his task by eleven— an hour after he had promised to be in bed—and then retired. Murphy, of course, was downstairs, waiting for his final run before joining Henry upstairs on the boy's bed.

Henry had no idea what time it was when the sounds in the yard awakened him. It took him a little while to realize that the noise was real; and, when he heard the sound of

174

glass breaking, he was sure that he was not dreaming. One look out the window told him all that he needed to know: Dogs were after the geese! He ran, shouting, to his parents' bedroom, but they had not returned. Something had to be done, but what? Call the police? No, the need was immediate!

He called his dog but the dog did not come. Murphy had crashed through the kitchen window to rescue his good, new friends, the geese.

The Beagle's escape was not a simple matter. He had clawed at the door and even tried to dig through the floor before jumping from floor to chair, to table and counter. Now only the window stood in his way. He hurtled sideways against it several times before crashing through. The snow on the ground cushioned his fall, and he was up and away in an instant—bleeding from three scratches. The Beagle was in action before Henry was down the stairs.

The boy didn't know where his dog was, but he knew where his father's shotgun was—in the hall closet. He found it, but he couldn't find any shells, and this time he didn't intend to be foolish. He stood on tiptoe and pulled everything from the shelf. Still no shells! He searched through the pockets of his father's old jackets, and found a single shell. It wasn't much, but it was better than nothing. Maybe, with luck, he could kill all the dogs with one shot.

His fingers shook as he placed the shell in the chamber. He pushed off the safety and ran through the house and out the kitchen door, shouting at the top of his lungs. The geese and the strange dogs were locked in battle. He saw two big dogs and a little black and white one, and he knew he couldn't get them all with one shot. One shot for one dog, he thought, and maybe the others will run away. One dog and maybe some geese. But there were already two dead geese in the snow, and he decided that there would be more even if he didn't shoot. All he could do was to aim and pray that he'd hit a dog and not the geese.

The war was all over the yard, and in the deep snow beyond. The boy brought the shotgun to his shoulder and tried to line the big black dog in his sights. And then he saw that there were four dogs, and the fourth dog was his Beagle! Now he couldn't shoot. How could he risk shooting his own dog?

Murphy didn't know that Henry was there. He had been extremely busy since he joined the fray by clamping his jaws on the first exposed flank that he saw. The flank belonged to Rover, and the yellow dog was too occupied to do more than rip a gash on Murphy's side before turning back to Walter Mitty. The sudden pain did not discourage Murphy; and, as the yellow dog ducked away from the gander's flailing wings, the little hound sunk his teeth into Rover's left hind leg. The Beagle was fighting for his family and home grounds. He did not stop to identify the invaders who were his old friends. He was wild with excitement, and simply doing his duty.

It was the Beagle's final contact with Rover. Mutt had never liked Murphy, and he wasn't sure if Rover's assailant was Murphy or not. It didn't matter to the mongrel. He was willing to fight, but not against the fat hens. Suddenly, here was somebody his size.

So Mutt ripped into Murphy, and the two engaged in a private war within the general war. They rolled over and over in the snow, with the big dogs and geese fighting all around them. Mutt was the quicker of the two, and his sharp, cutting teeth tore the Beagle in a dozen places. Murphy had the heart for battle, but not the experience. When his jaws found the mongrel, he held on. Mutt wasted no time. He believed in scoring often, and was at a disadvantage only once —when Murphy latched onto his collar and wouldn't let go. Mutt's attack was stalled. But then the old collar broke and he was free again to punish Murphy.

King and Rover paid no attention to the private war. They were locked in combat with enemies who fought in strange ways. The fat hens that they wanted to eat were apparently trying to eat them.

Henry could only stand by and watch from a distance as the geese and the big dogs traded blows. The Beagle and the little mongrel were somewhere out there in the deep snow, but he caught only fleeting glimpses of them. He was completely unaware that the fight had suddenly gone out of his hound. Murphy was bleeding badly for the second time that month. His recently recovered stamina had drained away, and Mutt, sensing total victory, kept up his cruel attack. The little mongrel was so eager for the kill that he lost all sense of caution and failed to notice the gander.

Three of the gander's wives were clubbing away at a very confused Rover, and Walter Mitty couldn't find room to operate. He heard Murphy whine right back of him. He looked and saw his friend the Beagle getting the worst of it from the black and white mongrel. Walter Mitty whistled and went to his friend's defense. He used his big bill with the efficiency of a rapier, and Mutt didn't wait to find out what was cutting him. The mongrel cried out in pain and dashed for safety—just as the battleground was bathed in sudden light. The carol singers had returned home, and the glaring headlights of their car exposed the whole, shocking scene. For a split second, the big dogs were immobile and the geese almost so. To Josie and George Deane, the sight that greeted their eyes was like a still life painting—except for the fleeing small dog.

"They're killing my geese!" moaned the horrified Josie. "George! No! Stay in the car! They'll kill you!"

She was too late. George was already out of the car. The big dogs were running into the night.

Neither of his parents had noticed Henry. The boy rushed to the car and clutched his father with his left hand. The shotgun was still in his right hand. He tried to speak but could only sob. He had controlled his terror for a long five minutes. Now there was no need for control.

"For heaven's sake," worried Josie. "Just pajamas, nothing on his feet, he'll freeze to death. Put him in here!"

George took the gun from the boy and helped him into the car. There Josie threw the auto robe around her sobbing, shivering son.

"Turn on the ignition and you'll get some heat," George directed. He stood outside the car. He saw that the safety on the gun was off, and shoved it on. Then he broke the gun and saw the single shell. Good Lord, he thought, what if the boy had slipped? One of us might have been killed!

Walter Mitty and what was left of his harem had waddled close to the car. The gander flapped his wings and stretched his neck and trumpeted his victory call. Then he and the females moved out of sight behind the house to continue their interrupted sleep.

George waited a few minutes—just in case the big dogs returned—then joined his wife and son in the car. Josie had calmed Henry, and the boy was able to talk. "He says there were at least three dogs in the pack. Two big and one small."

"I wanted to shoot, I really did," Henry explained. "But

first I was afraid I'd kill the geese, and I didn't want to shoot our Beagle."

"Our Beagle?" asked George. The boy didn't seem to be making sense. "Did you let him out of the house?"

"No, he got out by himself, through a window, somehow. I heard glass breaking."

"There's a dog now!" said Josie, simultaneously.

George got out of the car, grabbed the shotgun and aimed at the dog. But he held his fire. It was Murphy.

The beaten warrior's legs were weak, and he paused every few steps to summon new strength. Then he sat down in the full glare of the headlights, and George saw that he was covered with blood, and that goose down was matted in the blood.

"Josie, you and Henry had better get into the house," George directed. "I'll bring the dog in." He said it flatly, the way he always said things when he was disappointed.

"He put up a great fight. I watched him," said Henry. Then he and his mother went into the house.

George leaned the shotgun against the car and picked up Murphy. "Why did you have to pick Christmas Eve?" he asked the dog. He asked it flatly.

"I don't want to go to bed until we know that Kris will be all right," Henry insisted. It was two o'clock on Christmas morning and permissible to refer to Murphy as Kris.

The boy could hardly keep his eyes open. He and Josie had administered aid to the Beagle since just before midnight. Now nothing more could be done until the vet came and nobody knew when that would be. They had phoned and phoned but there had been no answer.

179

The wounded war veteran was resting. All of his cuts and gashes had been washed to prevent infection, and the serious bleeding had been stopped. In Josie's judgment, the dog was not so badly off as that other time, for his head was unmarked and his eyes were clear. She had given him some of the left-over brown medicine, and he had resisted a little—but not for long. His hospital bed was in the kitchen. The laundry basket was lined with towels—old towels this time. He was resting, but he was not comfortable, and he whimpered now and again.

"Please go to bed, Henry," Josie requested for the tenth time. "I promise to call you just as soon as we reach the vet."

"Be sure," said the boy, and he gave the Beagle a final pat before leaving the room. He started up the stairs, then stopped. What was the medicine that Art Purdy always gave his dogs when anything happened to them? Of course! Whiskey!—"Nature's medicine for man and beast," according to Mr. Purdy.

Henry turned and hurried down the stairs. He didn't know if his mother would approve of giving the Beagle a touch of whiskey, but it would do no harm to suggest it. The boy wanted to give the dog every possible first aid.

He heard the back door close and his father's voice saying, "Well, at least four of the geese are dead, and the yard is a mess of bloody tracks and feathers. And it's snowing again and everything will be covered by morning. Did Henry go to bed?"

"Yes, finally," the boy heard his mother say. "And he hasn't changed his story. He still says that his dog was fighting the other dogs and trying to protect the geese."

Henry stopped right outside the kitchen door. The words he had just overheard increased his anxieties tenfold. The

180

boy's worries about his dog's condition were suddenly secondary to fear—the fear that his dog would be taken away, for obviously his parents thought that the Beagle had turned bad. What could he do to convince his parents? He had told them the truth, over and over. What more could he do? He didn't know. So he just stood there, out of their sight, feeling miserable and helpless. And he listened.

"I keep reminding myself that we've never known Henry to lie, so why should he lie this time? Perhaps the little dog we saw running away wasn't the Beagle. If this one is guilty, if he really did rejoin his pack, why did he come running back to us?"

"Because he was in no condition to run very far and he knew it, I suppose. Now, I'm not saying that Henry lied to us, Josie. I think he's telling the truth about what he saw—but he was standing off at least fifty feet from the action, and how well could he see in the dark? I'm afraid he saw only what he wanted to see; he certainly didn't want to see his dog destroying your geese."

"He was the only witness, George."

"Not quite. You and I thought we saw the Beagle running away, and we certainly saw him return—all covered with evidence. I can't dismiss what everybody has been telling us: Pack dogs are smart, very smart, and they just can't be reformed. And this one is so smart that he came right back to us tonight, Josie. We didn't punish him the other time he tangled with the geese, and he must have reasoned we wouldn't punish him this time, either. We helped him before, so why not this time? Just look at him. Look at his eyes. Innocence personified. Is he a dog or an actor?"

"You sound like a lawyer."

"Sorry. I'm trying to sound realistic, and hoping that you

181

and I can face the facts and not be misled by sentiment again. We can't take any more chances with this one, Josie. We'll have to get rid of him. Now, for heaven's sake, don't cry."

His admonition came too late. Josie was weeping for her son, and for the dog, and for a personal failure that she could not define, but all she could say was, "And I thought . . . this would be . . . our best Christmas ever."

"We'll make Henry understand somehow, and we'll get him another dog. Come along, Josie. We can't stay up all night." George waited, but Josie didn't move. "All right," he said, "I'll try phoning the vet just one more time." He stepped into the hallway and came face to face with his son. "Henry! I thought you were in bed!"

The boy put his head down and said, "I couldn't sleep."

The lawyer put one hand under the boy's chin and tilted his head up and decided, "You've been crying, too. You heard what I just said to your mother?"

Henry nodded, but he wouldn't look at his father.

"It has to be this way," said George Deane, his tone was as gentle as he could make it. "We agreed in the beginning, remember? If the Beagle ever turned bad, we couldn't defend him forever, and we'd have to get rid of him, remember? We'll get you another dog, I promise."

The boy brushed past his father and ran to his dog. Tears rolled down his cheeks, but his voice was firm as he stood above the basket and pointed at the Beagle and almost shouted, "Look, Look! Can't you see? Why won't anyone understand?" Then he dropped to his knees and patted the Beagle, and the little hound gave his hand a weak lick.

George Deane tried to make sense out of his son's words,

but his legal training—even his paternal experience—failed him. He just walked to Henry and stood there, confused.

The boy turned his head and looked at his mother. "You remember that other time, Mom?" he asked. "How the wounds looked that other time? The big cuts were even ones, weren't they?"

Josie thought for a moment, and then she nodded. She left her chair and went to her son, and knelt by his side as he carefully pulled off the adhesive tabs holding the big bandage on the Beagle's left side. The red stained cloth covered the biggest cut of all—the one that Rover's teeth had slashed and ripped.

Henry worked slowly, and the Beagle whimpered. Then the bandage was off, and Josie leaned forward and examined the cut. It was ugly and deep, more of a jagged gash than a cut. Its edges were torn and uneven, and tiny pieces of flesh were missing.

Josie twisted her head and looked up at George. She tried to say something, but she was fighting tears and smiling, both at the same time. She couldn't say a word.

"You and your mother have discovered something, and I'm completely in the dark," confessed George. "What is it, Henry?"

Henry pointed to the wound and said, "This was made by something with teeth. It couldn't have been made by a goose's bill, Dad."

The lawyer knelt on the opposite side of the basket and looked closely at the wound. Then he asked, "Are they all like this?"

"All, except for a few scratches made by glass," the boy told him.

George Deane grinned. He reached over the basket and shook hands with Henry. "A brilliant defense," he said. "Congratulations. You are the best lawyer in the Deane family."

The tears started rolling down Henry's cheeks again, and Josie wept openly. The tears of both were born of joy and relief.

"Thanks, Dad," whispered Henry. They were the only words he could summon, the only words necessary.

The senior lawyer patted the dog, then Henry's shoulder, then his wife's. Next he straightened up and walked from the room, and when he returned he was wearing his overcoat and hat. He strolled to the back door and stopped there, then made a great show of putting on his gloves in a nonchalant manner.

Josie rubbed her eyes and asked, "And just where do you think you're going at this hour in the morning?"

"Oh, just thought I'd drive around here and there until I found the vet," said George. "Don't wait up. I'll bring him back. And by the way, Merry Christmas to the three of you."

From that day, Murphy answered to the name Kris. Nothing in his manner ever indicated that he missed or remembered his friends of the old days—those other vagabonds, King and Rover and Mutt. There would be times when he would half-bark and move his paws and stern in his sleep, but how does one interpret a dog's dreams?

The happy Beagle never knew that the pack's winter retreat at the lake had been discovered. The ice fishing was exceptional in February—the best in twenty years, according to Art Purdy—and George and Henry both caught their share of five pound pickerel. But it was other fishermen who noticed the tracks at the shallow end of the lake, where there were only a few frame cottages. They were the ones who told the sheriff about the huge paw prints, and he was the one who organized the search party. It took the searchers three days to finally sight the pack and their guns brought down Rover and Mutt.

King was wounded, and from the blood they found alongside his escape tracks in the snow, the men were sure that the big black one had died, too. But neither they nor anyone else in Green Valley ever found the body, and King's death remained presumed.

When spring came and the snow melted, George Deane found an old, torn dog collar just beyond the yard. It was a collar for a small dog, and the nameplate carried the name Mutt and a New Jersey address. It really didn't matter, but it was evidence that Henry had told the whole truth.

Months later, on the evening of the Fourth of July, the Deane family and Kris went to the lake to watch the annual display of fireworks. While they waited for the first barrage of rockets, Henry and Kris walked out on the dock in search of the best possible viewing position. They were watched by a group of summer residents, and one of them—a stout woman—approached Henry and asked if the Beagle was his dog.

"Yes," said Henry.

"Is your father a farmer?"

"No, my father is a lawyer."

"Oh, I used to have a dog who looked just like this one. The very same markings. Mine was smaller, of course. He was just a puppy. May I pet your dog?"

"Of course."

The stout woman leaned down and patted the Beagle's head and asked, "What's his name?"

"Kris," Henry told her. "Kris with a K."

"That's a very nice name. I called my dog Murphy. Do you know something, little dog? You look like Murphy's twin brother."

The hound suspected that Henry and the woman were talking about him, but no one will ever know if he remembered the name Murphy or even the stout woman. But he did give her hand a little lick, which may have meant something.

Kris or Murphy? The Beagle really didn't care what his name was, or how it was spelled. Now, a name was the least of his possessions.

A Roman candle shot into the night and exploded a shower of stars. The boy and the dog ran to the edge of the dock. There Henry kneeled, put his arm around the Beagle, and watched the sky.